Her mouth softened beneath his and he increased the pressure

With a tenderness he would never have believed himself capable of, he kissed Maggie. The experience was everything he'd imagined. Beautiful. Innocent. Breathtaking.

His arousal escalated. Why now? Why this woman? Ending the kiss, he whispered, "Night, Maggie," and walked off into the dark. Frustrated. Hopeful.

And still alone…

Dear Reader,

These are turbulent times in the world, and not a day goes by that I don't read or hear of conflicts around the globe. One evening on the news I saw a special report on the Walter Reid Army Medical Center in Washington, D.C. I wondered about the soldiers who returned from combat bruised and battered, physically and mentally. The news report sowed the seeds for *In a Soldier's Arms*.

Every man and woman who has fought, sacrificed and suffered for their country deserves a Happy-Ever-After. But often the enemy follows the soldier home. For some soldiers it's not the physical injuries but the psychological wounds that are most difficult to overcome. Abram Devane hopes to find peace and solace in the Heart of Appalachia. He doesn't expect to encounter a woman who makes it her mission to break him out of his self-imposed prison.

I hope you find Maggie O'Neil and Abram Devane's journey toward their very own Happy-Ever-After one filled with hope, trust, courage and—most important—love.

If you have a soldier story to share, I'd love to hear it. Drop me a note at marin@marinthomas.com or visit me on the Web at www.marinthomas.com.

Best wishes,

Marin

W gr
m

In a Soldier's Arms
MARIN THOMAS

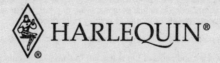

TORONTO • NEW YORK • LONDON
AMSTERDAM • PARIS • SYDNEY • HAMBURG
STOCKHOLM • ATHENS • TOKYO • MILAN • MADRID
PRAGUE • WARSAW • BUDAPEST • AUCKLAND

ISBN-13: 978-0-373-75204-1
ISBN-10:   0-373-75204-0

IN A SOLDIER'S ARMS

This edition published by arrangement with Harlequin Books S.A.

® and TM are trademarks of the publisher. Trademarks indicated with
® are registered in the United States Patent and Trademark Office, the
Canadian Trade Marks Office and in other countries.

www.eHarlequin.com

Printed in U.S.A.

ABOUT THE AUTHOR

Typical of small-town kids, all Marin Thomas, born in Janesville, Wisconsin, could think about was how to leave after she graduated from high school.

Her six-foot-one-inch height was her ticket out. She accepted a basketball scholarship at the University of Missouri in Columbia, where she studied journalism. After two years she transferred to University of Arizona at Tucson, where she played center for the Lady Wildcats. While at Arizona, she developed an interest in fiction writing and obtained a B.A. in radio-television. Marin was inducted in May 2005 into the Janesville Sports Hall of Fame for her basketball accomplishments.

Her husband's career in public relations has taken them to Arizona, California, New Jersey, Colorado, Texas and Illinois, where she currently calls Chicago her home. Marin can now boast that she's seen what's "out there." Amazingly enough, she's a living testament to the old adage "You can take the girl out of the small town, but you can't take the small town out of the girl." Her heart still lies in small-town life, which she loves to write about in her books.

Books by Marin Thomas

HARLEQUIN AMERICAN ROMANCE

1024—THE COWBOY AND THE BRIDE
1050—DADDY BY CHOICE
1079—HOMEWARD BOUND
1124—AARON UNDER CONSTRUCTION*
1148—NELSON IN COMMAND*
1165—SUMMER LOVIN'
        "The Preacher's Daughter"
1175—RYAN'S RENOVATION *
1184—FOR THE CHILDREN **

* The McKade Brothers
** Hearts of Appalachia

To the men and women in uniform who give their
lives to protect our freedom.

Chapter One

Maggie O'Neil loitered outside Scooter's Café in Finnegan's Stand, Kentucky, working up the nerve to enter the restaurant and inquire about her maternal grandmother—a woman she'd never laid eyes on in all her thirty years. The urge to climb into her car and drive back to Louisville was so powerful her stomach churned with nausea. Rarely did she react to stress physically. After years of being a nurse practioner, her nerves were strong.

She fingered the envelope in the pocket of her hot pink blazer. The letter, already a month old, was barely legible. Maggie had had to enlist the aid of her nursing colleagues to decipher the chicken scratches—incomplete sentences, misspelled words and bizarre phrases such as "It don't make me no nevermind," "Pert neer," "layin' up" and "Lans-sake." In the end, her coworkers had determined that the message had been a request for Maggie to return to her deceased mother's birthplace to retrieve the personal possessions left behind when her mother had run away at the age of seventeen.

Maggie had agonized over one sentence in her grandmother's note: "I'm yer only kin on yer mama's side left." And the signature at the bottom of the page: Margaret O'Neil.

Maggie's mother, Catherine O'Neil, had never married Maggie's father, but the two had lived together until he'd perished in a car accident when Maggie was a toddler. The desire to learn more about the woman Catherine had detested, yet had named her daughter after, and the need to discover if her father's relatives remained in the area, had driven Maggie to pack a suitcase and head for Heather's Hollow, her mother's birthplace.

The small town of Finnegan's Stand, not far from the hollow, boasted a main street of wooden storefront businesses dating back to the early 1900s—a post office, hardware store, beauty salon and Scooter's Café. A gas station and convenience store sat at the end of the street. For a Saturday afternoon, there was little foot traffic. No wonder her mother had felt trapped in this isolated mountain community. Maggie had been born in Louisville, gone to college at the University of Louisville, then landed a nursing job at a satellite clinic sponsored by Baptist Hospital East. In short, she'd lived her entire life in a large city, with movie theaters, shopping malls and chain restaurants at her disposal.

Sweat trickled between her cleavage, but Maggie resisted the urge to rub the front of her blouse. She wanted to blame her overheated body on the weather, but the sunny September day was on the cool side due to the town's higher elevation in the Appalachian Mountains. Her nervousness stemmed from the prospect of meeting her grandmother for the first time. Would the old woman be pleased to see Maggie or barely civil? Caught day-dreaming, Maggie didn't notice the café door open.

"Howdy, miss." The greeting came from a lumber-jack in a flannel shirt, scruffy jeans and a stained baseball cap. He flashed a tobacco-stained leer. *Eeew!* A wind gust sent the fine layer of sawdust clinging to his shirt dancing around his head.

"Ya lost or somethin'?" Holding a brown paper sack, its sides soaked with grease, sawdust man paused, his attention shifting between her face and her bosom.

Maggie edged backward until the window pressed against her spine. "You wouldn't happen to know how to get to Heather's Hollow, would you?"

A grimy finger pointed up at the slop of trees behind the town. "Take the road that forks off at the end of the street. Once ya cross Periwinkle Creek, yer in the holler."

"Great." She smiled her thanks.

He leaned forward, his cigarette-scented breath blasting her in the face. "I got time to show ya the way afore I head to the mill."

"Ah, no thank you. I—"

"We could have ourselves a little picnic." He held up the greasy bag.

A sliver of apprehension raced across Maggie's shoulders. She'd arrived in Finnegan's Stand less than ten minutes ago and already the small-town charm was losing its appeal. "Ah—"

"The lady said *no.*"

Maggie spun and collided with a solid wall of muscle. Hands grabbed her upper arms to steady her. Dressed in combat fatigues and a green T-shirt, which showed off well-defined biceps, the man—make that warrior—towered over her five feet six inches. She craned her neck and studied her rescuer's chiseled face.

He had a square jaw, high cheekbones, crooked nose and dark slashing eyebrows that showcased chocolate-brown pools of misery.

Startled by her assumption that the man possessed a wounded soul, she shifted under his probing stare. Her ability to sense things about people had always troubled Maggie. Once, she'd asked her mother about the thoughts that popped into her head, but her mother had attributed the condition to Maggie's overactive imagination.

A single eyebrow lifted at the outer corner, and Maggie's face warmed with embarrassment at having been caught gaping. She faced the mill worker, who appeared ready to bolt. "Thank you for the offer, but I have a few errands to run in town," she lied. With a nod, the man shuffled across the street and disappeared into the hardware store.

Before Maggie had the opportunity to thank the soldier, he slipped into the café. Surreptitiously she watched him claim a seat at the lunch counter, leaving his broad back to her. Something in his gaze had called to Maggie. As if feeling her attention on him, he glanced over his shoulder. Instead of the loneliness and emptiness that had been in his eyes moments earlier, the message he flashed now was loud and clear—*No Trespassing*.

Startled, she shifted sideways out of view. She blamed her interest in the man on the fact that she'd been involved with an enlisted soldier years ago. But after Michael had been shipped to Afghanistan, where he'd died during his unit's first patrol, she'd sworn off military men. No matter how sexy, strong or handsome, a man in uniform was nothing more than a heartache waiting to happen.

The post-office door opened, snagging Maggie's attention. An elderly woman with long silver hair marched down the sidewalk. Dressed in somber clothing—an ankle-length black skirt, navy blouse and a black jacket—the granny toted a rifle.

Was carrying a firearm in plain view legal? The woman climbed into a truck that should have found its way to a junkyard years ago. The engine sputtered, died once, then roared to life with a *bang!* Expecting her to drive at a snail's pace, Maggie gasped when the old biddy blew through the stop sign at the end of the street and sent the truck fishtailing as she swerved left and disappeared around the bend in the road.

I understand why you took off, Mom. The place was full of kooks.

DAMN.

At the squeak of the café door, the muscles along Abram Devane's shoulders twisted into a giant knot. The woman with the bewitching green eyes and midnight-black hair strolled toward him. He studied her reflection in the stainless-steel shelving across from the lunch counter. He'd bumped into her kind before— femmes fatales who fawned over men in uniform, then cut out when their perfect warriors arrived home not so perfect. Forcing his gaze back to the menu, he feigned interest in the daily special of meat loaf and mashed potatoes.

Clip, clop. Clip, clop. Clop. She paused about a foot away. Too close for comfort. Her intriguing scent drifted over his shoulder, reminding him of an activity he hadn't experienced in a long, long time—sex.

A feminine voice floated into his ear. "Excuse me. I

hate to bother you." She slid onto the stool next to him, evidently not hating to bother him enough to leave him alone.

Bracing himself, he cranked his neck sideways and made eye contact. *Yep.* He hadn't been mistaken. She was a knockout.

Green eyes blinked. "I'm searching for a Margaret O'Neil."

Betty Sue, where the hell are you? he wondered. The waitress had disappeared. Abram had made few acquaintances since arriving in the area a month ago and mostly kept to himself. The locals—excluding the stunning brunette next to him—respected his privacy. "Don't know a Margaret O'Neil."

"Oh."

Her simple utterance grabbed Abram by the gut and yanked. Just like a woman to insert the right amount of helplessness in a single word to guilt a man into rescuing her.

"You must not be from around here, either," she stated.

"Nope." Abram had been born and raised in a small Ohio town. He was staying—well, hiding out—in a former army buddy's cabin. If he hadn't had the need for a few groceries and the taste of real coffee, he wouldn't have made the trip into town today. After ten years in the military, he still struggled to brew a decent pot of coffee. Once a week he trekked into Finnegan's Stand to treat himself to Betty Sue's Colombian roast.

The woman next to him fidgeted, her earthy musk scent—like that of a belly dancer he'd watched perform in Jordan a few years ago—wafting past his nose.

Sigh.

Her whispered assertion drew his eyes to her mouth.

Full lips painted with the barest hint of red shine. Lips that begged for a man's mouth to cover them. A man's lips to lick them…his teeth to nibble them…his tongue to thrust between them. She was by far the most striking woman he'd ever encountered—which said a lot, seeing how he'd observed his share of exotic beauties throughout his military career.

A beautiful mouth combined with olive skin and high cheekbones hinted at a Native-American heritage. Although at first glance her hair had appeared black, under the flourescent lights, hints of auburn popped. Her eyes captivated him most, their expressiveness reeling him in like a fish.

"Thanks for your help outside." When she smiled, Abram swore flecks of gold flashed in the glittering green orbs.

Intrigued, he wondered if her eyes changed color when a man was deep inside her. The notion didn't shock him. After the things he'd experienced in the army, a passing sexual thought about a relative stranger was the least offensive.

Just then, Betty Sue stepped out of the kitchen and the tension drained from his body.

"Coffee?" The waitress set a cup on the counter and began pouring.

"Thank you," the black-haired beauty answered. Abram detected a hint of a southern accent, but nothing heavy like that of the old-timers in the area. She'd probably grown up in the city.

"Our cashier quit yesterday." Betty topped off Abram's mug. "I got folks to ring up before I take your order." She set the pot on the warmer, then cut across the room to the register near the door.

The stool beside him spun and the woman's knees bumped the side of his thigh, sending a zap of awareness through his body. "Maggie O'Neil. I'm from Louisville, but my mother grew up here."

City girl—he'd guessed right. "Abram Devane," he muttered, hoping she'd accept the hint that he wasn't interested in conversation.

"My mother passed away several months ago and I received a letter from my grandmother asking me to…" She shook her head, the motion sending her long locks swishing across her shoulders. "I'm sure you don't care to hear about my problems."

Smart woman.

With another heartfelt sigh, she faced forward. "As soon as I collect my mother's belongings, I'm heading back to civilization."

In Abram's opinion, civilization wasn't all it was cracked up to be. Odd, but the knowledge the beauty wouldn't be hanging around after today didn't produce the feeling of relief he would have anticipated.

"Apologize for the wait." Betty Sue loosened the pencil from behind her ear and tapped the order pad.

"No problem." Maggie smiled. "I'm searching for a relative in the area."

The pencil and order pad disappeared into an apron pocket. "Who's your kinfolk?"

"Margaret O'Neil."

"Granny O'Neil?"

"I'm Maggie, her granddaughter."

"Got a granddaughter, does she? Ain't that nice."

"Oh, no, it's not like that. We've never met."

Betty Sue frowned and Abram did his best to ignore the conversation. He'd met the infamous granny, but hadn't known her name was Margaret O'Neil. If he were the old bat's granddaughter, he'd tuck tail and skedaddle. While Betty Sue and the beauty next to him engaged in conversation, Abram intended to slip away. He gulped the rest of his coffee, unconcerned the hot liquid scalded his tongue. Like the rest of his body, his mouth possessed a thick hide, too. He tossed a five-dollar bill on the counter and left his seat.

"A passerby mentioned that Heather's Hollow is located on the other side of a creek. I don't recall the name."

"Periwinkle," Betty Sue supplied, then shouted across the room, "Hey, Abram. You headin' to yer cabin?"

Damn. He'd almost made it to the door.

"Will you show this here lady the turnoff to the holler?"

Double damn. "Sure." The sooner Maggie O'Neil got what she came for, the sooner she'd leave. The sooner he'd put her out of his mind—or attempt to. Once Abram had left the army, he'd discovered his biggest disability had been his memory and his inability to forget.

He held open the café door, but instead of brushing past him, Maggie O'Neil paused at his side, the top of her head even with his shoulders. "I'm ready." Her white-toothed smile blinded him.

That was one thing he'd never be—ready for the likes of Maggie O'Neil.

MAGGIE WAITED IN HER CAR while Abram Devane crossed the street. The hitch in his step suggested a war wound or possibly a sports injury. She blamed her curiosity on her medical profession and her inherent desire to fix people, not on his handsome face or sexy body.

Several college professors had encouraged her to enroll in medical school, but she lacked an essential ingredient found in many successful doctors: detachment. Instead of an M.D., she'd earned a master's degree in family practice. Once she passed the national board exam she became a Certified Family Nurse-Practitioner—a perfect fit for her, since she invested a lot of herself in her patients. For good or bad she was the kind of NP who cared for her charges heart and soul—laughed with them, cried with them and mourned with their families.

Her escort hopped into an older-model Jeep, pulled away from the parking space, then drove slowly down the street. Unlike the old woman who'd blown through the stop sign, the soldier obeyed the law. She followed as he navigated the winding ribbon of road. The higher they climbed the slower their speed. The blacktop was barely wide enough for two lanes and after a hairpin curve she understood the reason for caution. Reckless driving would send a vehicle plunging off the side of the mountain.

Four miles had passed before the Jeep's brake lights flashed. He stuck an arm out the window and pointed across the top of the vehicle. Peering through the windshield, Maggie spotted a rickety bridge. While she contemplated the safety of the structure, Abram put the Jeep into park and walked back to her car. She lowered her window and he leaned down.

"Heather's Hollow is on the other side of the bridge," he rumbled in her ear.

"The bridge looks a few hundred years old."

"It'll hold. Just be careful and go slow."

"Will do. Thanks."

He nodded, spun on his boot heel. After he climbed back into the Jeep, he edged forward past the entrance to the bridge, then stopped. That was nice of him— waiting to make sure she got across safely.

She clutched the wheel and inched the car onto the first plank. A few more feet and the rear tires rolled onto the bridge. *Nice and easy...* When the Honda's tires hit solid ground, she expelled a gust of air and glanced in the side mirror. The Jeep was still there. She waved out her window. At her signal, Abram drove off.

Now what? She should have asked Betty Sue the exact location of her grandmother's home. Hoping she'd spot *O'Neil* on a mailbox, Maggie drove on.

After five minutes of navigating the twisting road, she'd yet to pass a single mailbox. Nor had she spotted a house. The residents of Heather's Hollow must have built their homes deep in the woods. She imagined her grandmother driving this road and wondered how the old woman managed not to send herself off the side of a cliff. This part of the Appalachia received its share of winter snowstorms. Who watched out for her grand- mother? Made sure she had groceries? Checked on her health?

Don't care, Maggie. It's not worth the heartache.

Hugging the edge of the pavement, she rounded another curve—and almost steered the car into the ditch when a small rusted-out rattletrap nearly sideswiped her. She was thankful when the other driver braked. Maggie lowered the window. "Hello." Her greeting garnered a suspicious stare.

"I'm Maggie O'Neil. Would you happen to know where Margaret O'Neil lives?"

Wariness drained from the woman's eyes and she smiled. "Well, I'll be. Granny's granddaughter. I'm Annie McKee. I live directly behind the heather fields that border Granny's property. She's up the road a ways. I'll lead you to the end of her drive."

Before Maggie could ask how the woman intended to make a U-turn, Annie McKee put the matchbox size car into reverse and spun in a circle. Maggie followed the blue vehicle to an unmarked dirt track, then Annie McKee honked and sped off. Maggie studied the narrow path that cut a swath through dense forest. The passageway possessed more ruts and holes than a pioneer trail.

"Here goes nothing," she mumbled. Good thing she wasn't claustrophobic, because trees and underbrush flanked the car on both sides and blocked her view of everything except the road ahead. Why would anyone in the twenty-first century want to live in such seclusion?

Moments before Maggie's butt went numb from the jarring potholes, a cabin popped into view. *Oh, Mom. You didn't tell me you grew up in a hovel.* When Maggie's mother had described her childhood home, she'd used words like *rustic* and *simple.* Of course, that had been over thirty years ago and possibly the structure had been in better condition then.

The cabin her mother had lived in was worlds away from the apartments she and Maggie had shared over the years and the condo they'd purchased together along the Ohio River. At first she'd questioned her mother's excitement at moving into the plain two-bedroom, two-bathroom unit. Now she understood. The condo was the nicest home her mother had ever occupied.

Since the cabin lacked a garage, carport, barn or any structure suitable for sheltering a vehicle, Maggie parked her compact car to the side of the path, where the dense underbrush all but concealed it. When no one came out of the home and no dogs bounded from the woods, she left the safety of the car. The cabin might not be much, but the sea of purple heather surrounding it was breathtaking.

Maggie followed the narrow stone trail that led to the front door. The cabin was built of logs that had weathered to an ash-gray, and despite several deep cracks in the wood, the structure appeared sturdy. A cement material had been used to plug the gaps between the logs, and someone with a talent for masonry had constructed a chimney. The unique placement of stone was a work of art.

Two windows, one on each side of the front door, had curtains hanging across them. There was no porch or overhang to protect a visitor from the elements. A rocker sat across the yard under the sprawling branches of a hundred-year-old maple. Her heart tweaked at the image of her grandmother rocking alone beneath the tree. There had been no mention of a grandfather in Margaret O'Neil's letter. She wondered when he'd passed away.

Before she knocked and announced her presence, Maggie decided to investigate the property. She walked around the side of the cabin, where more heather fields greeted her. And smack-dab in the middle of the flowers… *An outhouse?* Yard art was all the rage these days. Maybe her grandmother had purchased the outdoor toilet as a decoration. A stone path led from a screened-in porch to the outhouse. Maggie circled the structure, smiling at the crescent moon carved into the door. She lifted the latch and peered inside. The smell wasn't as bad as she'd expected, but she found it difficult to imagine her mother had grown up having to use an outhouse.

Chest heavy with sadness, Maggie left the hut. She wished she knew more details of her mother's childhood. But any mention of the subject over the years had brought a pained expression to her mother's face, and after a while, Maggie had quit asking questions.

From her vantage point in the yard, she spotted an electrical line connected to the house. If the cabin had electricity, maybe her grandfather had installed indoor plumbing after her mother had left. The screened-in porch had been constructed from two-by-fours, not logs, suggesting it had been added years after the cabin was built. She strolled closer and peered inside. A crate of colored-glass bottles sat in a corner. A metal tub that resembled a livestock tank rested against the far wall. A shiver racked her body at the thought of bathing on a porch in the middle of winter.

"Ya plannin' to break in, or just droppin' by fer a look-see?"

Maggie twirled and gasped—*the old lady from the post office!* Maggie hadn't been known what to expect the first time she met her grandmother, but she hadn't anticipated staring down the barrel of a shotgun. Inching her hands into the air, she pleaded, "Don't shoot." The gun remained trained on her. "Would you please point that thing in a different direction?"

"If'n I decide not to shoot ya."

"You must be Margaret O'Neil. A woman named Annie McKee said I'd find you here."

"What business ya got with Granny?" The old

woman squinted, her eyes swallowed up by the folds of wrinkles wreathing her face.

"I'm your granddaughter, Maggie O'Neil." Even if the old woman wasn't half-blind, she might have trouble accepting Maggie was her granddaughter, since Maggie didn't resemble her mother accept for the green eyes. Evidently the females in the O'Neil family carried the gene for green eyes.

Hunched shoulders slumped as the old woman lowered the weapon. The glazed expression on her face alarmed Maggie. "Are you feeling poorly, ma'am?"

The craggy frown her grandmother flashed would have made a bridge troll think twice about scaring the next passerby. "Decided to show up, did ya?"

Maggie hadn't counted on much of a welcome, but the little girl in her who'd grown up without a grand-mother had hoped for a smile or a hug. There wasn't a soft spot anywhere on Margaret O'Neil—not in her stance, not in her expression, not in her voice and es-pecially not in her eyes. "I'll pick up my mother's things and be out of your way, *Grandmother.*"

"Name's Granny. Don't answer to nothin' else." The woman shuffled past Maggie, then paused at the porch door. "Least I knows Amaday Blackfox was yer Daddy."

Left to stand outside alone, Maggie steeled herself against the raw emotion that roared through her blood. She didn't like her grandmother—not one bit. The old biddy was mean-spirited, cranky, rude and— *She knows who your father is.*

"Ya comin' or not?" Granny bellowed. For such a frail woman, she possessed a pair of iron lungs.

If Maggie wanted to learn about her father's family and possibly their whereabouts, then she'd have to put up with the cantankerous geriatric awhile longer. "On my way, *Grandmother!*"

Chapter Two

BLACK. PITCH. RAVEN. Asphalt.

Abram stood outside the tiny cabin he'd called home the past month, compiling adjectives that aptly described the color of Maggie O'Neil's hair. His callused fingers had ached to reach for a long, shiny strand, to discover if the mass was as velvety as it had looked under the café's fluorescent lights.

He wondered how Maggie's reunion with her grandmother was going. Restless, he glanced at his watch for the tenth time since he'd driven off after Maggie's Honda had crossed the bridge over Periwinkle Creek.

A minute past noon, but it felt like midnight to his body. After two years of five to six days a week, ten to twelve hours at a time patrolling Baghdad, Abram knew his internal clock was busted. When he'd first arrived at the cabin, he'd spent his days chopping wood, making repairs, clearing fallen tree branches—everything and anything to exhaust himself. The strenuous work hadn't helped. Sleep came in snatches—brief periods of blissful unconsciousness mixed with tormenting dreams.

Nightmares of Iraqis reaching out, begging him to keep them safe from the violence, to chase the bad guys from their neighborhoods. Much of the time Abram and his unit had been successful, with minimal carnage, and had gone back to base feeling damn good about helping the locals.

He recalled the old widow who'd been kicked out of her home by rebels. Her neighbors had reported the incident to Abram, and one night he and his men had paid the enemy a surprise visit and reclaimed the woman's home for her. By her toothless smile one would have thought he'd given her Middle East peace instead of a two-room concrete hovel riddled with bullet holes.

Inevitably, though, his dreams shifted from helping the innocent to killing the insurgents, and then ended with a replay of the fateful afternoon he and his men had been lured into a trap. The price had been more than Abram could ever have imagined. Not only had he lost good, decent men, he'd lost a part of himself that day.

Once he'd received a medical discharge from the army, he'd wanted to find a hole, crawl inside and shut the world out. When the parents of one of his fallen comrades had gifted Abram their fishing cabin and the two hundred acres surrounding it because it held too many memories of their deceased son, Abram had jumped at the chance to hide in the isolated Appalachian Mountains.

Maggie O'Neil threatened his intention to remain in seclusion. He wished that it had been only Maggie's body that had snagged his interest. But in truth, he'd detected a vulnerability in her that cried out for protection—his protection. That he'd wanted to be her hero had caught him by surprise. He was done saving people. He'd found out the hard way that being a hero wasn't all it was cracked up to be.

He blamed his military training and time in Iraq on his urge to protect the innocent. But deep down he believed his reaction to Maggie had been more involved. When he'd stared into her green eyes, he'd found himself wishing for a normal life—marriage, family…a real home. Except, happily-ever-after wasn't in the cards, so if he understood what was best for him, he'd keep away from Maggie O'Neil.

A scuffling noise put his senses on high alert—an adrenaline rush associated with days, weeks, months of being the target of sniper fire. His gaze zeroed in on a section of underbrush fifty yards in the distance, where Mr. Raccoon's eyes gleamed gold.

Standing on its hind legs, the animal sniffed the air but made no move toward the apple cores and steak fat Abram had dumped on the ground. The pest wasn't bothered by Abram's presence. No surprise. Since leaving Iraq, he hadn't been a threat to anyone but himself.

"Go on. Eat and get lost."

As if the critter understood the command, it scurried to the garbage pile. Abram refused to admit the reason he tossed food scraps into the woods each day was that he was desperate for companionship—even if it came in the form of a four-legged scavenger. He'd been positive isolation was what he'd wanted when he'd quit his rehabilitation program. But used to the constant company of his military unit, he didn't know how to be alone.

And there was something else. After years of wearing forty-five pounds of gear, firing precision-

optic, fully suppressed, 7.62-caliber death bringers—
called Boom-Sticks—and patrolling in Humvees on a
daily basis, the prospect of living in his hometown in
Ohio and putting his accounting degree to work held
little appeal.

One thing for certain, though—numbers made
sense; war didn't. If he computed correctly, he obtained
the right answer. In war, he followed his commands,
carried out his orders to perfection, but the result
differed each time. His analytical brain struggled to
make sense of a war in which the line between good and
bad, right and wrong, often blurred. In which a soldier
was unable to identify the good guys from the bad guys.

Unbidden, Maggie O'Neil's face flashed through
his mind again, ending his musings of war. Man, what
he wouldn't give for a night in her arms. He suspected
she had the power to make him forget the past, if only
for a few hours. Maybe tonight his dreams would be
colored with the green of Maggie's eyes and not the
blood and gore of war.

Dreams or no dreams, his encounter with Maggie a
short time earlier reminded him that he needed to plan for
his future. The night might lay claim to his soul, but the
days belonged to him. He'd been mulling over the idea
of building a hunting lodge on the property. Tomorrow
he'd head into town and speak with Betty Sue at the café.
She might have a lead on a local construction company.

And if he was lucky, he'd catch one more glimpse
of the exotic, black-haired, green-eyed beauty Maggie
O'Neil.

MAGGIE WASN'T SURE what to expect when she entered
her grandmother's cabin, but it wasn't the pleasant,

cozy feeling that welcomed her. Her gaze was drawn to the massive stone fireplace centered in the far wall. The chimney was impressive, if not extraordinary, and a Dutch oven had been built into its side.

The cabin consisted of one main living area and a smaller room, which she assumed was her grandmother's bedroom. Multicolored rag rugs covered the plank flooring, and handmade afghans decorated the two chairs facing the fireplace and the rocker snuggled into the corner near the front door. The kitchen—circa *Little House on the Prairie*—comprised a rust-stained porcelain tub with double drain boards and a cast-iron pump handle. Good Lord, her grandmother cooked, cleaned and bathed with well water.

An apartment-size refrigerator occupied one wall, proving the cabin had functioning electricity. Shelves filled with pottery had been nailed to the wall next to the sink, and a small table with two chairs rounded out the space.

What interested Maggie most was the large piece of furniture to the right of the fireplace. The unit resembled a dining-room hutch…sort of. The top half contained shelves filled with glass jars; the bottom half narrow storage compartments. Maggie inched closer and studied the labels on the drawers: chickweed, blackberry, elder, dogwood, horsetail, goldenrod, ginger, wild yam, yarrow. The jars and bottles held herbs and salves. Her eyes wandered higher. Crammed onto the uppermost shelves were worn leather-bound journals, and she shoved her hands into the pockets of her blazer to keep from reaching for the dusty books. She wondered if the yellowed pages held secret cures, potions…maybe even spells. Her gaze traveled higher, then— *Yuck!* Her grandmother didn't use leeches, did she?

"Ya done snoopin'? I got Catherine's—yer mama's— things right here." Gnarled hands held a paperback novel and a necklace.

That's it? Maggie had driven over three hours to retrieve a book and a piece of jewelry? Her grandmother placed the items on the kitchen table, then shuffled to the sink and cranked the pump handle until water ran from the spout.

Was the water even safe to drink? Maggie wanted to ask if the wells in the hollow had been tested by the state, but kept quiet. A vision of her mother popped into her mind. Catherine O'Neil had escaped the hollow as a teenager and had lived the rest of her life in a large city with indoor plumbing and city-purified drinking water. Her grandmother had spent all her years in the mountains in less-than-ideal conditions and at the age of—

"How old are you?" Maggie blurted.

"Seventy-seven."

At the age of seventy-seven, the old woman was alive, whereas Maggie's mother had succumbed to cancer. Maybe well water wasn't such a bad thing.

Her grandmother dumped a handful of coffee grounds into a dented pot, filled it with water, then hung the handle on a hook inside the fireplace. Next, she poked the cinders, then added kindling from the woodbox, and a few moments later a small fire crackled.

"Ya hungry? I got bread made fresh yesterday and strawberry preserves."

Maggie's stomach rumbled in answer.

"Sit." A gnarled finger pointed to a chair at the table.

Arguing that she wished to be on her way crossed Maggie's mind, but she yearned to discover more about her father's family. And if she was honest with herself, she'd admit the old woman who'd driven Maggie's mother to flee at such a tender age intrigued her.

From the few stories she'd been told, Maggie had created a larger-than-life picture of her grandmother— a fierce, big-boned, brutish woman wielding a switch. The old lady slicing bread possessed a withered little body that would topple under a brisk wind. Her grandmother's movements hinted at a deep sadness, and Maggie was convinced her grandmother's bravado was forced at best. The passage of time, a difficult life and the loss of a child had left its mark on her face, with its deep wrinkles, sagging skin and age spots.

"Thank you," Maggie murmured when her grandmother set bread slathered with jam on the table. A mug of coffee followed. "Aren't you eating?"

The old woman sat across from Maggie, cradling a cup. "Been feelin' a might puny lately."

Her grandmother's comment nagged Maggie, which surprised her. She might be related to the woman, but they had no connection. She should feel no responsibility for her welfare—at least, that was what her subconscious argued. "How long has your appetite been off?" Purely a professional question, which Maggie attributed to her being a nurse.

"Since ya done sent the letter tellin' of yer mama's passin'." Her grandmother lovingly stroked the cover of the book she'd retrieved.

Maggie believed the bond between a mother and child was one that not even distance or a falling-out would sever—as evidenced by the fact that Maggie's mother had reached out to her parents when Maggie had been a child. Sadly Maggie's grandparents had never reached back.

Granny interrupted Maggie's musings. "Ya said cancer."

"Ovarian cancer." Her grandmother waited expectantly, so Maggie explained. "By the time Mom figured out something was wrong with her, it was too late. During the operation to remove her ovaries, the doctor discovered that the cancer had spread to other organs. He closed Mom up and sent her home." Maggie blinked at the sting in her eyes. She never had difficulty discussing the clinical aspects of her mother's condition, but saying "Two months later, she died" caused her great pain.

Every day Maggie lived with guilt because she hadn't sensed her mother's health problems. Her ability to pick up on things in others had failed with her own mother. "One evening we were dining out, and when Mom stood to leave, I noticed blood on the seat of her pants. I rushed her to the hospital, and after several tests she was diagnosed."

When her grandmother made no comment, Maggie finished the story. "I asked Mom why she hadn't had a routine physical for years, and she confessed that she didn't trust doctors." Maggie's blood pressure escalated at the memory. She'd never guessed her mother had harbored reservations about modern medicine. That Maggie had pursued a nursing career must have bothered her mother terribly, yet she'd never expressed any disappointment in her daughter's choice.

Face pasty white, Granny whispered, "Did my Catherine suffer?"

Her Catherine? Maggie wanted to argue that Catherine was more *hers* than her grandmother's. *What's the use, Maggie? Mom's dead and no amount of bickering will bring her back.*

Yes, Catherine O'Neil had suffered. The high doses of pain medication had kept her unconscious, and they'd said their goodbyes almost twenty-four hours before her mother had slipped away. The part of Maggie loyal to her mother wished to blurt the painful details of those last weeks, but Maggie didn't have the heart to wound an old woman whose grief for her daughter appeared genuine. "Mom took plenty of medication to control the pain."

With a curt nod, her grandmother left the table and disappeared into the bedroom. While Maggie awaited her return, she studied the novel, *Anne Frank: The Diary of a Young Girl.* Her mother had scrawled her name inside and the well-worn pages had yellowed with time.

Had her mother identified with Anne Frank? In a way, Catherine had been a prisoner in this tiny cabin.

The book's cover blurred before Maggie's eyes as an overwhelming sadness engulfed her. Young girls should also have read fantasies, happily-ever-after tales, like the stories Maggie had treasured as a child. Sliding the book aside, she fingered the silver necklace—a charm of a wildcat pawing the air.

"Clan Macpherson," her grandmother announced when she approached the table, eyes red-rimmed and puffy.

Keeping her gaze averted, Maggie tried not to gawk, but clearly her grandmother had left the room to cry, too proud to grieve in front of her granddaughter. Maggie figured the old woman had trouble expressing any emotion save orneriness. "What kind of clan?" Maggie asked.

"Yer mama didn't tell ya 'bout the clan?"

Maggie shook her head.

"A woman ought to know her kinfolk," Granny muttered. "Yer ancestors come from the clan Macpherson. The elders sailed from Scotland in the early 1700s. Settled these mountains in 1733. Yer mama's pappy is from a long line of masons."

"Did my grandfather build the fireplace?" Maggie nodded at the fixture.

"No. Yer ancestors done built the cabin and laid the stone fer the chimney round 1873."

"This cabin is a hundred thirty-five years old?" Wouldn't termites have eaten it to the ground by now?

"Land sakes, no. A twister done blowed it over in 1910 but the fireplace survived. Yer great-papaw rebuilt the cabin round 1912."

"What's a papaw?"

"Yer mama didn't teach ya nothin' 'bout nothin' up here, did she?" Granny's voice dripped with disgust.

Unable to answer without hurting the old woman's feelings, Maggie stayed silent.

"*Papaw* means granddaddy."

"Then the cabin is ninety-six years old?"

"Nope. Fire burned the second one to the ground in 1936." When Maggie's eyes strayed to the fireplace, Granny left the table and motioned up the side of the stone. "The fire caused that there crack. Yer papaw and his daddy built this here cabin in 1941."

Her grandmother's home was sixty-seven years old. More amazing was that the stone fireplace had survived a hundred thirty-three years. The fireplace should be registered with the Kentucky National Historical Society.

Questions clamored inside Maggie's head, but the day was fast slipping away. If she intended to leave the hollow before dark, she'd better speak up. Maybe after she had time to absorb today's visit, she'd return to the hollow at a later date. "You said you knew who my father was."

Mouth puckered, Granny resembled a withered apple. "That boy could yak a hound dog off a meat truck."

"Grandmother, I don't—"

"Name's Granny." The glint in the old woman's eyes dared Maggie to call her anything else.

"Granny, my father died in a car accident when I was three."

As her grandmother digested the news, Maggie speculated again whether she'd made the right decision in coming to the hollow. She'd return to Louisville and her life would go on, while her grandmother stayed behind, miserable and alone. She questioned what Granny did to keep busy all day. As much as she wanted to believe her grandmother deserved a lonely life after turning Maggie and her mother away years ago, Maggie was concerned about the old woman.

"Grandmoth—I mean, Granny," she continued, "do you know where my father's family lives?"

Her grandmother shook her head. "They's gone now. Done packed their bags and moved on. After yer mama run off, yer papaw took the shotgun over to the Blackfox cabin. If 'n the man had been home, he woulda shot Amaday's daddy clean through the heart fer not stoppin' the boy from takin' our Catherine away."

"Amaday?" Her mother had called Maggie's father Amad.

"Yer daddy's name was Amaday Blackfox. He was part Cherokee. Catherine called him Forest Water 'cause it riled yer papaw somethin' fierce." Granny's mouth curved in a wry smile. "Yer papaw didn't trust him."

"So you're all the family I have left?"

"Catherine was my only child. Tried fer years, but all my babies was stillborn. Don't know nothin' 'bout Amaday's kin." Her grandmother fingered the silver wildcat charm. "Yer papaw's been gone nigh on twenty-three years. You and me's all that's left."

Anguish filled Maggie at the knowledge that her grandmother had lived alone in this cabin for far too many years. How different all of their lives would have been if Maggie's mother and grandmother had found a way to forgive each other.

"Ya ain't hitched?" Her grandmother nudged Maggie's bare ring finger.

"Came close, but he was killed in action in Afghanistan."

"A soldier, was he?"

Abram Devane's face popped into Maggie's mind. The man was the quintessential soldier—handsome, strong and, she sensed, brave. Very brave. Maybe if Abram had been the soldier to ask her to marry him, she would have said yes.

Forcing her thoughts from Abram, she informed her grandmother, "His name was Michael. We met in college. After he graduated, he entered the service." She waited for her grandmother to murmur something sympathetic, but the old woman's mouth remained closed. Had her grandmother been this *hard* all her life?

"How do ya get along?"

"You mean, how do I support myself?" At Granny's nod, Maggie answered, "I'm a nurse-practitioner. I work in a family-practice clinic."

"I'll be hog-tied and snickered bottomed."

"Excuse me?"

"I'm the clan healer," Granny boasted with a smile.

Clan healer. Maggie's gaze shot to the cabinet against the wall. So her grandmother practiced holistic medicine.

"I patch up folks, 'cept I don't have no doctor tellin' me what to do or any of them fancy medicines that cost an arm and a leg." The sarcastic statement told Maggie exactly what the old biddy thought of modern medicine. She tried not to take offense, but she would have hoped her grandmother might be proud her granddaughter had followed in her footsteps—sort of.

"Better be on my way." Maggie stood, ignoring the prick of guilt at leaving after such a short visit. When she got back home, she'd call her grandmother to check on her… Maggie surveyed the cabin. "Do you have a telephone?"

"Don't have no phone. Got me a bell on the porch. If 'n I need help, I clang it."

Oh, brother. Maggie would have to drive three hours if she wanted to make sure her grandmother was well. How likely was that to happen? At least she'd made this trip to Heather's Hollow. Not all her questions had been answered, but that was okay. Some things were better left alone.

"Thank you for the—" she glanced at the uneaten piece of bread on the table "—for my mother's things." She was halfway to the front door when the sound of crunching metal screeched through the air.

Maggie dashed outside and up the stone trail, then skidded to a halt. A truck had rear-ended her car, shoving the front bumper into the tree Maggie had parked in front of.

"Laws a-mighty!" Granny exclaimed when she joined Maggie.

A redheaded woman close to Maggie's age hopped out of the truck and gasped, "Oh my God! I'm sorry. I didn't realize you had a visitor, Granny." The woman inspected the damage and grimaced.

Attempting to process what had occurred, Maggie didn't budge from the stone pathway until a little red head popped into view through the passenger window of the truck. Her medical training kicked in and she hurried toward the pickup. "Are you okay, sweetie?"

Big blue eyes gaped.

The imp was adorable. Hoping to distract her, Maggie asked, "Honey, are you hurt? Did you hit your head?" She brushed the riot of curls aside and checked the miniature forehead for bruising. "Are you a leprechaun?"

Giggles erupted from the petite mouth. "Mama says I'm her little leprechaun. And my daddy calls me Katie bug 'cause it rhymes with ladybug."

The leprechaun's mother wrung her hands. "I am so sorry. I took my eyes off the road for just a second and then *bam!*"

Granny shuffled near and inspected the front bumper. "Dad gum, that don't look good," she muttered, before making introductions. Maggie, this here is Jo Macpherson and her youngin', Katie."

Jo offered her hand. "Macpherson was my maiden name. Granny forgets I'm married. It's Jo Mooreland."

"Nice to meet you. I'm Maggie O'Neil, Granny's granddaughter."

The other woman's mouth formed an O before she snapped it shut. "I'll pay for the damages."

"I have insurance," Maggie assured her.

"What brung ya out here, Jo?"

Jo switched her attention to Granny. "Sullivan and I were hoping you'd watch Katie. The school is closed Monday for Labor Day and he booked a room at the Gambill Mansion in Blaine to work on our book. We'd planned to arrive back here Monday afternoon." Jo glanced at Maggie. "But you have company—"

"Oh, I'm not staying," Maggie said quickly, then winced when her gaze strayed to the front end of the car. "At least, I hadn't intended to."

A flash of jealousy zipped through Maggie at the look Jo and Granny exchanged. What did it matter if her grandmother had found a replacement granddaughter over the years? Jo Mooreland was nearly Maggie's age, so naturally the two women had clicked.

The day was fast becoming one of the worst Maggie had experienced in some time. She faced her grandmother. "Would you mind if I stayed with you until I made arrangements for my car?"

Granny's eyes skirted over Maggie before settling on the rocking chair under the tree. "Don't make me no never mind."

What does that mean? Was she or wasn't she welcome? "If you'd rather I slept at a motel—"

"I'm sure Granny would love for you to visit a spell," Jo interjected.

A noncommittal grunt escaped the old woman's mouth.

Throat tight, Maggie cursed herself for allowing her grandmother's less-than-enthusiastic attitude to bother her. Rest assured, as soon as the Honda was drivable, she'd hit the road. She studied the leprechaun, who hung out the window, swinging her hair against the side of the door. At least the child would provide a diversion from Granny's crotchety demeanor. "All right then. I'll remain until my car is fixed, and I'd be happy to help my grandmother care for your daughter."

"Granny usually stays at our cabin when I leave the hollow, but I suppose Katie—"

"Do you have indoor plumbing?" Maggie interrupted.

Jo's deadpan reply would have been believable had her eyes not glittered with humor. "Yes, we do," she answered solemnly.

Maggie noticed that her grandmother appeared to be more interested in poking her knobby finger through the hole in the cuff of her blouse than in the conversation around her. "My grandmother and I will be happy to watch Katie at your place."

"Great." Jo hustled over to help her daughter out of the truck. They hugged and kissed, then Jo hopped into the vehicle and called through the open window, "I'll stop by Tom Kavenagh's place and ask him to tow Maggie's car to the gristmill. If anybody can fix it, Amos can."

Her car would be repaired at a gristmill by a man named Amos?

"Welcome to Heather's Hollow, Maggie." With a wave of a hand, Jo Mooreland drove off, leaving Maggie alone with a smashed car, a grumpy granny and a child whose eyes sparkled with devilment.

Chapter Three

In Maggie's opinion, Jo's cabin was everything she imagined a rustic vacation home should be—modern appliances, including a washer and dryer; indoor plumbing; lots of privacy; even an authentic, if not slightly askew, tree house. If the home hadn't been constructed of logs, it would have fit into any of the middle-class suburban neighborhoods surrounding Louisville.

Maggie stood at the kitchen sink, washing lunch dishes as she kept an eye on Katie in the backyard. Granny snoozed on the couch. Evidently folks in the hollow didn't make a fuss over Labor Day. Back home, Maggie's coworkers had already boarded the *Belle of Louisville*—the oldest operating steamboat in Kentucky. The clinic doctors chartered the vessel each year for the medical staff and their families. The *Belle* sailed along the Ohio River until dusk, when it dropped anchor for a fireworks display over the water. This would be the first year since beginning her job at the clinic that Maggie wouldn't be attending the festivities.

Tossing aside the dish towel, she left the house, cut across the yard and called through the branches of the maple tree, "Mind if I join you, Katie?"

"Okay. But you have to duck 'cause this is for little people. My daddy always hits his head."

"Thanks for the warning." Maggie scaled the foot-holds nailed to the trunk, then crawled inside the tree house on her hands and knees. "This is very nice," she complimented Katie, sitting cross-legged. "I like the fluffy pink rug." Katie snuggled a doll in her lap.

Until now, Maggie had never felt deprived that she'd been raised in apartments. She imagined how different her childhood would have been had her mother not run off with her father. She would have grown up among friends and grandparents, with a forest for a playground and maybe a tree house like this one. "What do you like to play?"

Narrow shoulders lifted up and down. "I pretend I'm a teacher like my mom, and sometimes I pick heather like Granny."

Whenever Katie mentioned Granny, Maggie suffered an odd twinge in her chest. *Jealousy?* She didn't want to admit she was envious of a six-year-old, but obviously Katie and Granny had a close relationship— a bond rightfully Maggie's. "What does Granny use the heather for?" Curiosity about her grandmother's home remedies prompted the question.

"She makes medicines," Katie answered.

Maggie recalled her grandmother's hutch and the numerous dark blue and light green jars on the shelves. Not sure how much longer she'd be able to sit inside the small enclosure without becoming claustrophobic, she offered, "Would you like to invite a friend over to play with?"

"My friend Sara has two daddies. But she can't play today 'cause she's visiting the daddy who lives far away." Katie fussed with the doll's clothes, all the while casting furtive glances Maggie's way. After a short silence, she whispered, "You wanna play a spy game?"

Sounded intriguing. "How do you play?"

"We can't play here 'cause *he's* not here."

"He who?"

"The person we're gonna spy on."

"Does Granny know you're a spy?" Maggie tweaked the child's nose, assuming the game was make-believe.

Katie's expression sobered. "Granny can't know 'cause she'll tell Mama, and Mama will get mad."

So the game wasn't pretend. She doubted her grandmother would approve of Katie pestering one of the neighbors. Maggie's position in the clan was tenuous at best. She didn't care to be accused of participating in delinquent activities with a child. "Let's find something else to do."

Katie's mouth formed a pout. *Stubborn imp.* "Who is this person you spied on?"

Nose scrunched, Katie answered, "Don't know. He's not one of us."

Maggie's father, Amaday Blackfoot, hadn't been a clan member, either. She believed her grandparents' disapproval of the teen had contributed to her mother's decision to leave home.

"I was going to pick mushrooms for Granny when I saw him."

"Where does he live?"

"Behind Granny's heather fields."

Maggie hadn't recalled her grandmother mentioning that her property bordered a stranger's. Concerned not only for Katie's safety but also her grandmother's,

Maggie insisted, "Spying on someone isn't polite, Katie, but maybe you should show me where he lives."

The little girl leaned forward and whispered, "You can't tell my mama."

Oh, honey, I can't promise that.

Katie didn't appear to be aware that her request had gone unanswered, because she tossed the doll aside and scrambled out of the tree house before Maggie had unwound her legs and crawled to the opening. Once her feet hit solid ground, Maggie announced, "Wait here while I tell Granny we're taking a walk."

Katie grabbed her sleeve. "Granny sleeps a lot. She won't wake up while we're gone."

Oh, boy. Jo probably had no idea her babysitter fell asleep on the job. "I'll leave a note so Granny won't worry if she wakes up."

When Maggie ducked inside, her grandmother's snores greeted her ears. She tiptoed across the room and studied the old woman, who looked frail and ancient in sleep. Was her constant napping a sign of failing health? Granny had probably never consented to a physical exam or a blood test her entire life. After scribbling a note explaining their whereabouts, Maggie headed outside and followed the little girl around to the front yard and the path that began at the edge of the property.

The dirt trail, barely wide enough for two people to walk side by side on, wound through trees, shrubs and thickets of dogwood bushes. After a few minutes they broke into a clearing and Maggie spotted her grandmother's cabin in the distance. She'd discovered a shortcut to Jo's home.

Skipping ahead, Katie called over her shoulder, "This way."

They crossed an open field before Katie veered onto another path, which returned them to the woods. Annie McKee, the woman who'd escorted Maggie to her grandmother's when Maggie had first arrived in the hollow, had mentioned that her property butted up to Granny's. "Is Mrs. McKee's house close by?"

"Ms. Annie lives over yonder." Katie pointed off into the distance, but surrounded by forest, Maggie had no idea if the direction was north, south, east or west. "This takes us to Granny's think box."

"What's a think box?"

"A place Granny sits and thinks, silly."

"Is it a real box?" Maggie teased.

"Nope." Katie flung her arms in the air. "It's a big circle that goes round and round and round."

Maggie hoped the "think box" was nearby. The forest sounds made her jumpy—unfamiliar bird squawks, scuffling noises and dark shadows. That Katie had traveled this distance alone, without telling anyone, made Maggie determined to speak to her grandmother about the child's excursions. After a bit of climbing, they arrived at the top of an incline. Katie motioned below. "See."

"Amazing." From her position above the valley, Maggie had an unobstructed view of what resembled a labyrinth. A long walkway flanked on both sides by a trellis, now overgrown with vines, led to the entrance. The circular pattern reminded Maggie of the Yellow Brick Road in the *Wizard of Oz* movie. Heather bushes bordered the winding path and she breathed deeply of the perfumed scent. "This belongs to my grandmother?"

Pointing at the stone bench in the middle of the

circle, Katie said, "That's where Granny sits while she's thinkin'."

Why had her grandmother created this ancient symbol on her property? Had this been here before Maggie's mother had left?

"Follow me." Katie scampered off with the energy of a playful squirrel.

Maggie wasn't so quick because her leg muscles rebelled at having to climb uphill. A thirty-minute walk three times a week with her coworkers during lunch breaks did little to prepare a body for trekking through the Appalachian Mountains. When they reached the top of the incline, the view snatched Maggie's breath. Far below, nestled in a grouping of trees, sat a tiny cabin and… A Jeep. The soldier's Jeep.

Although she wasn't one hundred percent certain about Abram Devane's character, Maggie's ability to sense people's intentions had never led her wrong in the past and her gut said Abram would never harm Katie. Regardless, she doubted Jo would approve of her daughter pestering him.

"I've met the man who lives there," she murmured.

Katie's eyes bulged. "You have?"

"His name is Mr. Devane."

Before Maggie had the opportunity to warn Katie to respect Abram's privacy, the cabin door opened. "Duck," Katie whispered. She yanked Maggie's pant leg and the two collapsed to the ground.

The soldier strolled outside, wearing fatigues, combat boots and nothing else. *Oh, my.* Even from a distance, his bulging biceps and six-pack abs elicited an appreciative sigh from her.

Bucket in hand, he crossed the property to the edge

of the woods and emptied the contents, then tossed the pail onto the porch and retrieved the ax on the step. As he headed for the chopping stump, the hitch in his gait was more pronounced than it had been Saturday, and Maggie wondered if that was because he thought no one was watching. She'd offer to examine his leg but doubted he'd allow her near him.

Heave-ho. *Smack.* Heave-ho. *Smack.*

His muscles bunched and jumped with each whack of the ax and she envisioned Abram in the heat of battle, his formidable body a force to be reckoned with. What was his story and why was he living alone in the mountains?

Katie made a game of counting the number of logs he stacked on the pile, while Maggie contemplated why, after a few strokes of the hatchet Abram stared into the distance as if lost in thought—*or just plain lost.*

Maggie shivered at the notion that flashed through her mind. Her ability to see inside people, to feel their pain and sense their purpose, was more a curse than a blessing. She had enough troubles of her own—her wrecked car, her chaotic feelings for her grandmother and her sudden confusion over who the real Maggie O'Neil was…a city girl who'd been raised by a single mom or a country girl from a Scotch-Irish clan in the Appalachian Mountains. Before arriving in the hollow, she'd been positive she was Maggie number one. Now that the shock of such a different environment had worn off she admitted that the simplicity of the Appalachian life fascinated her.

This was one time Maggie should listen to her instincts. No matter that the soldier was handsome, sexy and intriguing, Abram Devane was a complication she didn't need right now.

"Thirty-seven," Katie counted when Abram tossed another log onto the pile.

"We'd better leave before he spots us."

"Let's say hello." Katie popped off the ground and shouted, "Hey, mister!"

Oh my God.

The ax above Abram Devane's head froze and his body stiffened. He scanned the woods.

Maggie glanced sideways, searching for a hole to crawl in. Abram lowered the ax and lifted his gaze to the top of the hill, where it landed on Maggie. She gleaned comfort in believing he was too far away to hear the sound of her breath whooshing from her lungs.

She expected a greeting. She received nothing. No wave, salute, not even a nod. He stood motionless…watching…waiting.

"He doesn't want to be disturbed and we're on his property," Maggie hissed.

"This is Granny's hill," Katie protested. "She grows mushrooms over there."

With great effort Maggie tore her attention from Abram's muscular torso and followed Katie's waggling finger to a damp, dark, recessed area several yards away. "Even so, we'd better let Granny's neighbor finish his chores."

"He doesn't care if we spy."

Maggie grabbed Katie's hand and tugged her down the hill. "Promise me you won't go off alone into the woods again."

"Why?" Katie skipped to catch up with Maggie.

"Because you could fall or get bitten by a snake or—"

"You're a scaredy-cat, huh?" The little girl giggled.

"I guess I am." Maggie stopped at the bottom of the hill, went down on one knee and looked Katie in the eye. "It's important you keep your word, honey. No walks alone in the woods. The next hike, ask an adult to go along."

"Okay, I will."

"Pinkie promise?" Maggie wiggled her pinkie finger and Katie grinned as she wrapped her smaller digit around Maggie's.

"Let's head back to your house. I have to borrow Granny's truck to drive into town and check on my car."

"Can I come?"

"Of course." Maggie was counting on the little chatterbox to distract her mind from sexy Paul Bunyan.

MUCH TO KATIE'S displeasure, her parents had arrived home minutes after they'd returned from Abram's. Whether out of a sense of loyalty toward her grandmother or the fact that she expected Katie's parents would accept the news of their daughter's forays into the woods better from a clan member than a relative stranger, Maggie opted to first inform Granny of Katie's activities.

The talk had been postponed when Granny retreated to her bedroom to take a nap as soon as they entered the cabin. The old woman was definitely sleeping too much. With permission to use the truck, Maggie headed into Finnegan's Stand to check on her car.

The tedious drive along the winding road offered Maggie time to ponder her grandmother. She suspected the woman's sleepiness might not be due to old age but to a specific medical condition. The past night when Maggie had brought up the subject of a physical exam,

Granny had thrown a temper tantrum a three-year-old would have envied.

Margaret O'Neil had insisted her body and teeth had gotten along fine all these years without a doctor or a jaw cracker. Her poor opinion of modern medicine had hurt Maggie more than she'd cared to admit. If truth be told, she had hoped the two of them might exchange medical remedies over the next few days while the Honda underwent repairs, and if permitted, Maggie intended to assist her grandmother with her duties as clan healer. At seventy-seven, Granny was too old to be planting and harvesting heather, collecting mushrooms or anything else in the woods, never mind spending her free time babysitting or doctoring her neighbors. Maggie wondered if her grandmother had considered seeking a helper.

Are you volunteering for a permanent position?

Startled by the idea, Maggie took the curve at the bottom of the mountain too fast and almost landed in a ditch outside Finnegan's Stand. Good grief, she had no interest in giving up her position at the clinic to help her grandmother *heal* people. She'd be a fool to trade the comfort of her condo for a cabin without a toilet. And she knew her grandmother would care nothing about Maggie's knowledge of medicine. After a few short months Maggie would be dying to leave—like mother like daughter.

What about Abram Devane?

Okay, so he was the one checkmark in the positive column. She certainly wouldn't mind becoming better acquainted with the soldier. Maggie had dated a few times over the years since Michael but had been too busy with her work at the clinic for any serious relationship, and then her mother had become ill and well, there had been no time for a man in her life. Abram made her miss a man's company. A man's attention. Maybe she'd stop by his cabin tomorrow and apologize for spying on him today.

She slowed the truck to a crawl as she drove through town. In honor of the holiday, one business was closed—the post office. The remaining stores were open, including Scooter's Café. At the end of the street, Maggie veered onto the dirt road that her grandmother claimed led to the gristmill. Off in the distance, partially hidden behind a hill, sat a two-story wood-and-stone structure. When she entered the lot, her pulse jumped at the sight of Abram's Jeep parked near the eighteen-foot water wheel.

What's he doing here?

The thought of meeting Abram again sent her pulse skyrocketing. After she parked the car, she glanced in the rearview mirror. Satisfied she didn't have food stuck in her teeth or dirt smudges from her hike with Katie, she walked toward the garage. Male voices floated through the open door, and she hovered in the shadows, not the least bit contrite about eavesdropping.

"These foreign cars got too many danged electronic gadgets," a grizzly bear of a man grumped as he pulled his head from beneath the hood of Maggie's silver Honda Civic Coupe.

Abram Devane studied the guts of the vehicle. "The engine block is damaged. A couple of pistons, the connecting rod and the crankshaft are mangled, too."

"Where'd ya learn 'bout engines?" the "bear" asked, wiping his hands on an oily rag.

"The Humvees in our unit were always having

problems in Iraq. Me and a couple of buddies spent our free time keeping them running."

"Well, I ain't touchin' this. Kavenagh shouldn't 'f brought the car here. Ought to be towed to a dealership."

The Honda belonged to Maggie O'Neil—the bewitching woman Abram had caught watching him earlier in the afternoon. "No one was hurt, were they?"

"Nah. Kavenagh said somethin' 'bout Granny's neighbor Jo hittin' the parked car from behind 'n rammin' it into a tree."

The rush of relief at hearing it confirmed that Maggie hadn't been hurt caught Abram by surprise. He'd barely talked to the woman, yet she'd managed to do what no other had since he'd left Iraq—make him care. He had a feeling Maggie had the power to wreak havoc on him if she got too close. "Insurance should cover most of the repair work," he said after a stretch of silence.

"Heard she's Granny's kin. Betty Sue said she ain't nothin' like the clan."

"What's that supposed to mean?"

"Most of 'em up there in the holler is red haired and hot tempered." The old fart guffawed, then added, "Heard she got hair the color 'f a witch's hat."

Maggie's hair might not be the bright red of the clan, but her green eyes shouted Irish from a mile away. "There's a hint of auburn when the sun bounces off her head." Abram winced when he realized he'd spoken the thought. At least he hadn't confessed that he fantasized running his hands through her locks, feeling the softness rub against his chest, or burying his nose in the mass. "Who's going to tell her the bad news?"

"Tell me what bad news?" Maggie O'Neil stepped into the garage.

Abram's gaze collided with Maggie's green-eyed stare and the same shock wave he'd experienced earlier in the day, when he'd spotted her on the hill above his cabin, traveled through him.

"Howdy, missy. Name's Amos." The grizzled owner offered a beefy hand.

Maggie shook his hand. "Maggie O'Neil." Then she flashed a smile that forced the air from Abram's lungs. "Hello, Abram."

God, she's beautiful. "Maggie." He nodded, concerned about how much of the conversation she'd overheard, specifically his comment about her hair. He didn't want her to know he found her attractive. Didn't want to give her that kind of power over him.

"Folks been talkin' 'bout Granny's kin showin' up out 'f the blue. Ya don't favor Granny none. 'Cept maybe in the eyes."

Instead of acting offended, Maggie explained, "My father was part Cherokee."

Abram had guessed right—Maggie possessed Native-American genes. The result was a striking woman.

Motioning to the mangled car, she said, "Looks like I won't be returning to Louisville tomorrow."

"Several parts have to be replaced," Abram said. "If you tow the car to an authorized body shop or Honda dealership, insurance should cover the cost of parts and labor."

While Maggie pondered the crumpled heap of metal, Abram pondered the two front teeth that nibbled her lower lip. For good or bad the woman forced his body to stand up and take notice. He tried to blame his physical reaction to Maggie on the fact that for the past three years he'd been diving behind buildings instead under the covers with beautiful women. He'd had offers to sleep with women since he'd come home from the war, but none had captured his interest. And that worried him, because he feared his physical attraction to Maggie could easily evolve into something more. If he wasn't in such sorry shape—physically *and* mentally—he'd be tempted to get to know the black-haired beauty better.

"May I use your phone to contact my insurance company?" she asked Amos.

"Help yerself." Amos nodded to an open door across the garage.

After Maggie left to make her call, Abram brought up the reason he'd sought out the gristmill owner in the first place. "Betty Sue said you might recommend someone in the area who does construction work."

"Might. Watcha gonna build?"

"I'm considering converting my cabin into a hunting lodge."

Amos frowned. "Ya mean yer thinkin' 'o rentin' it out to hunters?"

"That's right."

"Clan ain't gonna be happy 'bout that."

"I'd post boundary markers around the two hundred acres so hunters wouldn't trespass on the clan's property." Amos continued to frown. Damn it, the cabin and the land were Abram's to do with as he pleased.

"Ya ought to be talkin' to Granny 'bout it first."

The old woman was the last person Abram intended to discuss anything with. In truth, he didn't need the income from a hunting lodge as much as he needed something to occupy his time and prevent his mind from wandering…remembering. Since enlisting in the army after graduating from college, he'd invested most of his military checks in a retirement fund. Ten years of pay added up to a tidy sum—enough money to do whatever he wished with the property.

Amos spoke when Maggie reappeared. "Well, missy?"

"My insurance company won't pay for a tow, but they'll cover the repairs minus a five-hundred-dollar deductible." A barely audible sigh escaped her parted lips and Abram steeled himself against the urge to gather her in his arms and assure her everything would be all right.

"Nearest dealership is in Pikesville and the emergency towing company I contacted charges four hundred sixty-five dollars to haul the car that far."

"Got me a truck with a hitch. Abram here could give ya a tow. I'd charge ya fer gas is all."

Abram winced at Amos's offer.

"You wouldn't mind?" Green eyes framed with long black lashes implored.

Oh, hell. "Is tomorrow soon enough?" Abram asked.

"Perfect." She smiled, flashing her white teeth. "What time should I meet you here?"

"You're coming along?" Spending four hours in tight quarters with the beautiful Maggie O'Neil would be pure torture.

Her raven eyebrows dipped toward her nose. "I'll have to sign the paperwork and show them my insurance information."

That made sense. Now, if only Abram could make

sense of the way his heart thumped wildly at the prospect of him and Maggie alone in the front seat of a truck. "Eight o'clock too early?"

"I'll be ready."

Not half as ready as I'll be.

Chapter Four

"Well, speak up, child," Granny ordered as soon as Maggie entered the cabin. "Amos gonna repair yer car?"

"Afraid not. It has to be towed to a dealership."

The knitting needles between Granny's knobby fingers stopped clicking. "What are ya fixin to do? Go home to Louisville?"

And miss the opportunity to spend the day with Abram Devane? Not! Maggie collapsed in the chair in front of the fireplace and attempted to contain her excitement about tomorrow's trip to Pikesville. She'd have Abram's undivided attention for several hours, and she looked forward to getting to know him better.

"When ya gotta be at yer clinic?" Granny's question interrupted Maggie's thoughts.

"I took the week off." After retrieving her mother's personal effects, Maggie had intended to use the remaining vacation days to paint the living room in her condo. *Hmm...* Paint the living room or spend the day with Abram—that was a no-brainer. Abram won hands down. "Granny, have you met the man who lives in the cabin that borders your property?"

Knitting needles clicked furiously again. "Ya mean the soldier who's been hangin' round these parts?"

"His name's Abram Devane. I ran into him Saturday at the café when I'd stopped to ask directions to the hollow. He offered to tow the Honda to Pikesville tomorrow."

"Ya best steer clear of that feller."

Surprised by the warning, Maggie confessed, "I'd planned to ride along with him."

"Can't trust a man who ain't from here."

Maggie condoned caution, but Granny's vehemence hinted at paranoia. Irritated by her grandmother's suspicious nature, she snapped, "Does that mean you don't trust me, since I wasn't raised in Heather's Hollow?"

Granny's silence stung. What did Maggie care if her grandmother trusted her or not? They might be related by blood, but they weren't close—yet. "Abram seems like a decent man." He might be a loner, but Maggie *sensed* a goodness deep inside him. Not to mention he was downright sexy and handsome. "We're leaving in the morning."

Granny's scowl told Maggie the old woman didn't approve of her granddaughter going off alone with a stranger. Time to change the topic to Granny's health. "I'd like you to see a doctor. Your frequent napping might be a sign of anemia." *As well as your irritable nature.*

"Can't an old woman rest her eyes 'afore folks claim she's sick? 'Sides, my nappin' ain't none of yer business."

Granny may have bullied Maggie's mother, but the cantankerous woman had another thing coming if she intended to treat her granddaughter the same way. "I'm concerned about your napping while watching Katie."

Eyes wide with hurt, Granny protested, "Ya sayin' I'm neglectin' that poor child?"

"Katie said you fall asleep a lot." Maggie didn't have the heart to tell the whole truth, so she settled for, "I'd hate to have Katie wander off and get hurt while you're napping."

Granny pursed her mouth but refused to make eye contact. "Resting after meals or late in the afternoon isn't uncommon for a woman your age," Maggie assured her. "But several naps a day could be a sign that you have an iron deficiency."

"Well, I ain't goin' to no crackpot doctor. He can't tell me nothin' I don't know."

Had her grandmother been diagnosed with an ailment? Confused, she asked, "What are you talking about?"

"That I'm gettin' old and old folks nod off from time to time."

Good grief. "A simple blood test is all you need. Where's the nearest clinic?"

"Don't matter. Can't go 'cause I ain't got no money."

"Your medical insurance should cover the cost."

"What insurance?"

Not surprised that her grandmother didn't have insurance, Maggie doubted she even received a social-security check. "I'll pay the doctor's fee."

"I ain't no chairity case. Been gettin' along by my lonesome fer years." Granny sent a narrow-eyed glare across the room. Maggie suspected her grandmother's defensiveness was a self-protective mechanism. She'd lost a daughter and a husband, not to mention the still-born babies she'd given birth to. And her granddaughter had no intention of remaining in the hollow, so why should the old woman reach out for help?

"Why doesn't Finnegan's Stand have a medical clinic?" Maggie asked.

"Most folks'round these parts ain't got extra money to pay a doctor."

"What about government programs—"

"The clan don't want the government's money."

"Why?"

"Government folks is always trespassin' up here, checkin' on the clan and stickin' their noses in our business. Promisin' us money if'n we do things their way. The clan don't want to change. We like us just fine the way we is."

Even though medical care in the hollow was a touchy subject with her grandmother, Maggie pushed. "What happens when you're no longer able to help others?" *Silence.* "Who will assist you then?"

"Ain't nothin' gonna happen to me. I'm fit as a fiddle."

No one lived forever. "Anyone besides yourself who's familiar with first aid?"

Following a long pause, Granny whispered, "No, just me." Then her grandmother's eyes brightened. "If'n ya stick round fer a while I'll show ya how to use heather fer healin.'"

The urge-to-heal obsession Maggie possessed thrilled to her grandmother's offer to learn about holistic medicine, but her practical side feared that forming a bond with the older woman would interfere with Maggie's vow to be faithful to her mother's memory.

Was it possible that Maggie's mother had been mistaken about Granny? After all, Catherine had been a teenager when she'd left home. Teens rarely saw eye-to-eye with their parents. What if Granny wasn't as cold as Maggie had been led to believe?

You'll never find out if you return to Louisville to wait for your car to be repaired.

Maggie had plenty more vacation time, and curiosity made her wish to learn more about her Scotch-Irish ancestry and the customs and traditions of the clan, even her grandmother's labyrinth.

Granny's yawn sealed Maggie's decision. The old woman wasn't getting any younger, and who could say when Maggie would visit again.

Don't forget Abram. Or his eyes…those deep brown pools intrigued Maggie. Underneath his soldier persona, she sensed a caring, compassionate man. She yearned to make him smile. To chase the shadows from his eyes.

Be careful, Maggie. She fretted over the damage Abram could do to her heart if she allowed herself to become close to him. Too bad she didn't possess the willpower to stop herself.

Forcing a note of enthusiasm into her voice, Maggie hinted, "I'd love to go with you when you visit your patients." She pointed to the hutch. "And I'm curious about the herbs in the drawers."

"I gots to check on ol' Jeb's hand. Put twelve stitches in it a few days ago."

Ouch. "When did you intend to drop in on him?"

"Day after tomorrow."

"Mind if I join you?" Before her grandmother protested, Maggie asked, "What should I cook for supper?"

"Got fresh-picked collard greens on the porch 'n leftover ham in the frigerator."

Maggie's eyes strayed to the blue yarn. "What are you making?"

"Baby bunting."

"Who for?"

"Katie's mama, Jo."

"Jo's pregnant?"

"Expect she will be shortly."

Maggie resisted the urge to ask how her grand-mother knew such a thing. Maybe Jo had confided in Granny that she and her husband were trying for a second child?

Or had Maggie inherited her ability to *see* things from her grandmother?

FIVE MINUTES IN the truck with Abram Devane and already Maggie fretted over her decision to tag along while he towed her Honda to the dealership in Pikes-ville. Eyes straight ahead, shoulders rigid, fingers stran-gling the steering wheel, he hadn't uttered a word since "'Mornin'" when she'd arrived at the gristmill shortly before 8:00 a.m.

"You're probably wondering why Katie and I were up on the hill above your cabin yesterday," she blurted, since he didn't appear to have anything to say.

If not for the way his jaw clenched, Maggie would have assumed he hadn't heard her. "My grandmother and I were babysitting the little girl, and Katie asked me if I wanted to play a spying game with her."

He glanced her way, his thick eyebrows forming a V. Abram's broad forehead, square jaw and wide mouth lent him a stubborn aura and the bump along the bridge of his nose suggested his sniffer had been broken more than once. He cleared his throat and she jumped at the rumble. Embarrassed that he'd caught her gawking, she continued, "I told Katie it wasn't safe to wander around the woods and she promised not to hike out to your cabin anymore."

"I'm not a child molester if that's what—"

"Of course you aren't," she assured him.

Her comment drew another sharp look from him. "You don't know anything about me."

If that wasn't a challenge, Maggie wasn't sure what was. "You're a champion for the underdog and a protector of people." She smiled at his wide-eyed gape. She refrained from giving details about her ability to sense things about people, lest he accuse her of being a psychopath.

"Thanks," he mumbled, flushing at her compliment.

"You're welcome." Maggie feigned interest in the purple asters growing along the highway. "What rank in the military were you?"

"Major. Why?"

"Your voice has an authoritative ring. I doubt any soldiers ever disobeyed you."

One corner of his mouth quirked. "Not if they understood what was good for them." He flipped on the radio to an oldies-but-goodies station as the truck zipped past a signpost proclaiming 85 miles to Pikesville. He switched the subject. "Are you arranging for a rental car today?"

"My insurance doesn't cover one." Maggie contemplated how she'd make it back Louisville if her Honda wasn't fixed by the time she ran out of vacation days.

The conversation exhausted, tension escalated between them until the air was thick and difficult to breathe. When Abram reached for the radio dial a second time, Maggie clamped her hand around his forearm, her heart skipping a beat at the spark that ignited between his skin and her fingertips. She'd touched him less than five seconds when he snatched his arm from her grasp.

Flustered, she muttered, "Don't switch the station. I like Elvis."

He shifted on the seat, leaning closer to his door.

Maggie suspected that had he been able to drive the vehicle standing on the running board, he would have. Irritated by the ridiculous awkwardness between them, she demanded, "Have I done or said something to offend you?"

His head snapped sideways, causing a popping sound in his neck. His brown eyes flashed before he returned his attention to the road and uttered a quiet, "No."

"Silence makes me nervous," Maggie admitted. "Because of my work, I'm used to hearing beepers, buzzers and children crying."

"What do you do?"

"I'm a nurse-practitioner. I specialize in family practice at a satellite clinic for Baptist Hospital East in Louisville." Was it her imagination, or did Abram's grip on the wheel tighten even more? "What branch of the military did you serve in?"

"Army."

"Retired or on leave?"

"Medical discharge." The skin over his knuckles threatened to split wide open.

Obviously he didn't care to talk about his time in the service, but Maggie was interested in his military experience, so she pestered. "Why did you join the army?"

"I'm not much of a conversationalist." He attempted an apologetic smile.

"That's okay. I'll handle the questions and one-word answers are fine." His lips twitched, making her yearn for a real grin. "I don't detect much of an Appalachian accent. Where are you from originally?"

"Ohio."

"College?"

"State."

"I attended the University of Kentucky at Louisville." When he made no response, she tried another question. "Did you serve in Iraq?"

"Fallujah. And Baghdad."

"I dated a soldier during college. He enlisted after he graduated." Michael's sweet, boyish features appeared before Maggie's eyes. "He proposed to me before he shipped off to Afghanistan." She paused, waiting for Abram's curiosity about her relationship with Michael. He didn't disappoint.

"And…?"

"I thought we should hold off, so I promised to give him an answer when he returned on his first leave." After all these years the memory of his marriage proposal hadn't faded. "He died the first week his unit went out on patrol."

"I'm sorry." The simple sentiment was more sincere coming from Abram than all the condolences she'd received from her coworkers and her mother.

"Lord, I did my best to talk Michael out of joining the military, but he'd decided to take advantage of the tuition repayment program the army offered."

"Why didn't you want him to enlist?"

"Because he didn't have the heart of a soldier. Being in the military was a means to an end—a way to erase his school debt. Deep down I doubted he'd make it back alive." Which made postponing their engagement unforgivable. Maybe if she'd said yes, he'd have paid attention to his surroundings. Instead, his inexperience had made him an easy target.

Abram cleared his throat. "How did he die?"

"Sniper bullet. I received his letter ten days after I learned he was killed on patrol."

The muscle in Abram's jaw ticked, but he kept his eyes on the road. "You said your mother grew up in Heather's Hollow, but you didn't?"

"My mother got pregnant with me when she was seventeen, and ran away to Louisville with my father. He passed away when I was three. It was just me and Mom until she lost her battle with cancer this past Christmas."

His brown eyes softened with compassion. "You've had it rough." After all the death and mayhem Abram had most likely experienced in the military, that he could sympathize with Maggie's pain showed a sensitive side she suspected he didn't wish others to witness.

"Any more relatives besides your grandmother?"

"Nope. Granny and I are all that's left."

He offered a half smile that flipped Maggie's heart. She doubted Abram was even aware of how much sex appeal he possessed. "Rough reunion?" he asked.

"You could say that. She won't accept me calling her anything but *Granny.*"

His smile drooped. "I've met your grandmother."

Why hadn't Granny mentioned that she'd spoken with Abram in person? "Then you're aware of how stubborn and opinionated she is." Maggie wiggled on the seat until she faced Abram, eager to discuss her grandmother with someone outside the clan. "Did she tell you that she's a healer?"

"Our conversation was brief. The day after I moved in, she pounded on the door and demanded to know if I was a squatter or if I had permission from the owners to use their cabin."

"That's my grandmother."

"I had made clear that the Monroe family had gifted me the cabin and the surrounding land."

"What was her reaction?"

He chuckled, the sound stilted, as if he rarely laughed. "She warned me to keep off her land and mind my own business."

"Do you intend to live in the cabin permanently?"

His eyes narrowed before he returned his attention to the road. "Haven't decided. Why?"

Yes, why, Maggie? She didn't dare confess that she found him attractive. Or that he was the first man in a long, long while she wanted to get to know better. Instead she said, "I noticed your limp. I'd be happy to examine your—"

"My leg is fine."

Maggie suspected the limb wasn't, but she admired Abram's courage. How many times had patients walked into the clinic complaining about the smallest discomfort? One man had been convinced he had a terminal disease. Several tests and hundreds of dollars later, the diagnosis had been intestinal gas.

Admiration aside, she assumed that Abram hoped she'd believe he wasn't interested in pursuing anything more than a casual conversation with her. He might have convinced her if she hadn't caught him casting sideways glances at her breasts when he thought she wasn't paying attention.

FOR THE PAST forty-five minutes Abram had waited in the dealership parking lot adjacent to the repair bays. From behind sunglasses he observed the manager on duty—Fred somebody—go over paperwork with Maggie as they stood next to the dented Honda.

Abram had offered to go inside with Maggie, but she'd politely declined. He'd expected her rebuff. He hadn't exactly been Mr. Conversationalist on the drive to Pikesville. If he was honest with himself, he'd admit he enjoyed Maggie's company, but after years of socializing with soldiers—mainly men—his social skills with women were rusty—particularly gorgeous women like Maggie.

Another ten minutes passed, and then Maggie shook the manager's hand and left. As she strolled across the lot, he noticed the pinched lines bracketing her mouth. "Bad news?" he asked when she stopped next to him.

"'Fraid so. At least a week if not longer, depending on the availability of parts. And the head mechanic is on vacation the rest of this week."

Her bottom lip quivered when she sighed and Abram had to stuff his hands into the front pockets of his jeans to keep from hugging her. He struggled for something to say, couldn't think of anything, so he opened the truck door for her. She crawled in and scooted across the front seat. He hated that Maggie was sad, and a part of him wanted to find a way to cheer her up. Find a way to prolong their time together. He wasn't ready to head back to Finnegan's Stand.

He cranked the truck engine, then drove out of the dealership parking lot. At the stoplight his eye caught the bannerlike advertisement for Stock-Car Race Week posted at the corner. He'd spotted the signs as they'd driven through town earlier. He hadn't been to a race since before he'd enlisted in the army. *What if...* As soon as the light switched to green, he spun around the corner, drove down the block and returned to the dealership parking lot.

"What are you doing?" Maggie asked.

"Be right back." He jumped out of the truck and headed for the receptionist in the main building. Five minutes later he had all the information he needed. Now he had to convince Maggie that watching a stock-car race was something every woman should experience once in her lifetime. Hopefully, attending the event would take Maggie's mind off her car woes for a while.

He poked his head through the open driver's-side window. "Ever been to a stock-car race?"

Maggie shook her head. "Why?"

"Pikesville's annual stock-car race is taking place all this week at Miracle Mile."

"What's Miracle Mile?"

"A dirt track." He'd be the envy of every man there if he walked into the event with Maggie on his arm. "You up for it?"

Her mouth curved in a slow smile that sent his blood pressure soaring. "Sure. As long as I'm stuck in Appalachia, I might as well experience all its charm and flavor."

He grinned until his cheeks hurt. He hadn't smiled like that in ages. "Then let's do it." He followed the signs for the event and a half mile outside of town he left the highway and drove down a dirt road. "Do you know much about stock-car racing?"

"Haven't got a clue."

"My eldest brother competed in several events. He was fifteen years older than me, so I never had the opportunity to go to the races. But he worked on his car in the garage, and I remember sitting in the front seat and pretending to drive."

The truck hit a rut and Maggie yelped when her backside lifted several inches off the seat. "What kind of car did he drive?"

"A 1976 black Nova Shark. He bought it from a salvage yard and rebuilt the engine." The road came to a T and Abram drove left into a gravel parking area. The track sat a hundred yards away, surrounded by a chain-link fence. The roar of revving engines filled the air.

"Wow. That's loud," she shouted, her eyes alight with excitement.

Abram decided that no matter what happened today, he was glad for this time with Maggie. "You don't happen to carry a set of earplugs in your purse, do you?" He wasn't concerned about protecting his ears. A loud car race was nothing compared with roadside bombs exploding and IEDs—improvised explosive devices—detonating.

Wiggling her fingers, she joked, "Plugs are right here." She motioned to the crowded parking lot. "Has the race begun?"

"The event lasts all day and into the night. Sounds like they're holding the heat races right now. Those are shorter runs around the track that determine the driver's starting position for the main event."

They left the truck, crossed the lot and stopped at a folding table manned by two young women wearing tight T-shirts and heavy makeup. Maggie opened her purse and Abram clamped a hand around her wrist. "You're my date. I'm paying."

One black eyebrow rose, then Maggie caught the girls ogling him and batted her dusky eyelashes. She moved closer and cooed, "Well now, sugar, I guess I am your date."

With a chuckle he set a twenty on the table, grabbed a brochure and caught Maggie's hand. Abram admitted that he played with fire flirting with Maggie, but he couldn't help himself. She was too perfect. Too good for him.

As they walked through the gate, Maggie nudged his side. "Does that happen a lot?"

He set a hand against her lower back and guided her past the concession stand to a seating area along the curve of the track. "Not as often as men drool over you, I'm sure." Abram counted seven guys he'd caught eyeing Maggie as they located their seats.

After a few minutes the cars coasted to their perspective pits, which were nothing more than empty spaces alongside the track. As soon as the raceway was clear, the attendants hosed down the dirt.

"Won't the water create mud and cause the cars to slide? Maggie asked.

"The track's made of clay and the best driving conditions are when the surface is tacky."

"How much money is at stake today?"

Abram opened the brochure and scanned the contents. "Looks like two thousand for first place."

Maggie wrinkled her nose. "That's not very much."

"This is a local race. Most of the drivers compete as a hobby, not a living. Bigger races pay out at twenty-five and fifty thousand."

A horn blew, signaling the drivers to take their positions. Maggie pulled his shirt sleeve and pointed to the starting line. "Now I know why this sport appeals to men." The woman holding the green flag looked as if she'd walked off the set of a *Dukes of Hazaard* episode.

"All part of the ambience." Maybe ten years ago, when Abram had been in his twenties, he'd have drooled over a woman like that. Not anymore. The kind of female he preferred was…*Maggie*.

As the cars revved their engines and the announcer introduced the drivers and their sponsors, Abram decided that at least for today he could pretend Maggie was his.

"How long does the race last?" she shouted.

"A hundred laps."

"What?" She tilted her head in his direction.

He took advantage of the loud crowd noise and leaned into her. Lord, she smelled good. Not even the strong odor of gasoline hanging in the air masked Maggie's sultry scent. He put his mouth against her ear and answered, "A hundred laps." Too caught up in her scent and the feel of her hair tickling his lips, he didn't immediately break contact. Of their own volition, his eyes closed and for a moment he blocked out the world, save Maggie.

She moved her head and he opened his eyes, their gazes colliding…their mouth inches apart…their breaths mingling…*BAM!*

Startled by the capgun blast to begin the race, he and Maggie jerked apart. Cheeks pink, she smiled shyly, then watched the cars circle the track. He followed suit, but his thoughts weren't on the race. Had he imagined the yearning in Maggie's green eyes? If the gun hadn't interrupted them, would he have kissed her? Would she have allowed him to?

At lap twenty-five, two cars bumped and Maggie clutched his thigh. The feel of her fingers digging into his muscle was pure ecstasy. If he was lucky, there'd be a bigger scare and Maggie would jump into his lap.

The two cars that bumped managed to stay on the track, and slowly Maggie uncurled her fingers from his leg. Abram wasn't even sure she was aware that she'd grabbed onto him. "Be right back." Requiring a few minutes to cool down, he headed for the concession stand. Bad idea.

When he returned, he found a young, wet-behind-the-ears stud with cut-off sleeves and tight jeans in his seat. As soon as the guy caught sight of Abram's glare, he shuffled back to his own seat several rows over.

"Thanks." Maggie accepted a hot dog and a soda from Abram. "That nice man was explaining the point system, but I still don't understand it."

He would have attempted an explanation, but he lost his train of thought when Maggie bit into the dog, chewed twice, then rolled her eyes and moaned. So much for a cooling down—his body temperature shot off the charts.

"I didn't realize how hungry I was. Thank you."

"You're welcome." Without noticing his actions, he rubbed the pad of his thumb against the ketchup stain at one corner of her mouth. Next time he'd buy her a Frito pie instead of a wiener.

As the cars zipped around the track all Abram could contemplate was how much he enjoyed being with Maggie. She made him feel like a normal guy—not a soldier. He forgot about his past. Forgot about his disability. He was just an ordinary Joe in the company of a beautiful woman—a woman who, if he wasn't careful, could become more of a threat than any he'd faced in Iraq.

Chapter Five

"Are ya familiar with horses?"

Maggie's subconscious heard her grandmother's question, but her mind was elsewhere—yesterday's stock-car race, Abram and their almost kiss. She absently pierced a piece of fried ham and subtly shook the fork to remove the thick, red-eye gravy clinging to the meat. Her grandmother had added coffee and flour to the pork drippings to create the tasty, high-caloric sauce for their breakfast.

What had kept Abram from kissing her? She had no doubts that he was attracted to her. Several times at the racetrack she'd felt his gaze on her face…not to mention other parts of her body. And what about the gentle brushes of his hand against her arm, her lower back and her wrist? His lips touching her ear when he'd whispered…?

"Ya home up there?" Granny bopped Maggie on the forehead with the back of a spoon.

"Ouch. What did you do that for?"

"Been starin' into space ever since ya got home from spendin' the day with that solider."

Time to change the subject. Granny made no bones

about the fact that she didn't like Abram, and Maggie wasn't in the mood to argue with her, so she changed the subject. "I've never been up close and personal with a horse. Why?"

"'Cause that's how we're gettin' to Jeb's cabin."

Maggie shuddered when she envisioned her grandmother tumbling from the saddle. A broken hip would be the least of Granny's injuries. "I didn't notice any horses on your property." Maybe the animals roamed the heather fields.

"Ain't got none. The clan blacksmith loans me his."

"Is there a way to arrive at Jeb's home other than on horseback?"

"Ya kin paddle up the Black River, then double back on foot the next day."

The next day? Camping in the woods had never been Maggie's idea of fun. As a matter of fact, staying in her grandmother's cabin was all the communing with nature Maggie intended to do. "Are the animals well-behaved?"

"Mine's long in the tooth."

What did that mean?

An hour later, Maggie saw her grandmother's horse—a swaybacked nag. Maggie's, on the other hand, was a spirited gelding. "He's awfully big," she muttered. Dark, black eyes filled with distrust observed her every move.

"Blue's a good fella. He'll do right by ya," Tom Kavenagh assured her as he saddled the horse outside a recently constructed barn. The new wood had been left to weather naturally, minus stain or paint.

At first glance the blacksmith reminded Maggie of the infamous pirate Redbeard. Compared with Abram, whose chest and shoulders were muscular and broad, Kavenagh's torso was double the size. But his quiet voice and gentle demeanor proved he was no swashbuckling threat.

"Up you go." He bent at the waist and cupped his hand near the stirrup. Maggie placed her foot in his grasp and he hoisted her in the air.

"Maybe I should sit sidesaddle like Granny," she suggested, when her inner thigh muscles protested at being spread taut over the horse.

"Only Raison uses a sidesaddle." Granny's small gray mare resembled a donkey more than a horse.

"This ol' boy knows the way." Tom patted Blue's neck. "Don't pull too hard on the reins, or you'll confuse him."

"Does he spook easily?"

"Not unless somethin' grabs him by surprise."

Sweat beaded her upper lip. "What do I do if he—"

"Land sakes, girl. Stop yer yakkin'. Ain't got all day." Granny clicked her tongue and headed for the far side of Kavenagh's property.

Body stiff and upright, Maggie kept a loose hold on the reins, but her thighs squeezed the daylights out of Blue's sides. Kavenagh swatted the horse's rump and Blue jumped forward, following Raison. "How far is Jeb's cabin?" she called after Granny.

"'Bout three miles."

Three miles there. Three miles back. *Ouch.*

Granny coaxed her horse into the woods and Blue trailed along the narrow path. The terrain appeared similar to the area she and Katie had hiked near Abram's cabin, yet Maggie got the impression they weren't anywhere near the soldier's home. The Appalachian Mountains had been in her backyard all her life, but neither she nor her mother had explored the area or visited the famous Cumberland Pass.

Worried the old woman might lose her seat, Maggie kept a watchful eye on her grandmother. After several minutes, she conceded that Granny was as content as a cat sunning in a window. Shoulders hunched, body swaying with the easy rhythm of Raison's gait, the old woman let her head droop as if she were catching a few winks.

Rubbing the twinges in her neck, Maggie wished she could relax. After what felt like forever, the horses emerged into an open field with two mobile homes. For an instant she believed they'd arrived at their destination. Then Granny ruined Maggie's euphoria by guiding Raison past the trailers and into the woods again.

Later—twenty minutes to be exact, because she checked her watch—the sound of rushing water reached her ears. Blue caught the scent and broke off the trail, deciding that he wanted a drink.

"Granny!" Maggie called, unable to halt the horse.

"Git back here. Yer goin' the wrong way," her grandmother called.

"I can't stop him!" Maggie ducked in the nick of time, just before a tree branch smacked her in the face.

"Jerk the reins!" Granny shouted.

Remembering Kavenagh's warning, Maggie applied a steady pressure. Snorting, the gelding halted, pawed the ground in disgust and flung his head from side to side. "Whoa, Blue. Thatta boy. Easy now."

Granny on Raison sidled up next to Maggie.

"Stubborn cuss. Might as well let 'em have a drink."
Granny stayed atop her horse as the mare approached
the streambed. Maggie followed suit, not sure she'd be
able to hoist herself up on Blue if she jumped off. The
horses stopped at the edge of the water and drank their
fill.

When they continued on their way, Maggie asked,
"What's the population of the hollow?"

"Three hundred somethin'."

"Katie mentioned that her mother was a school-
teacher."

"Jo teaches the youngin's in the holler. Her granddaddy was an elder. Someday she'll be one, too."

"What does a clan elder do?"

"Makes decisions fer the clan. We're all gettin' older
and there ain't many who's willin' to carry on."

"Why's that?"

"Most young folk don't care nothin' 'bout the old
ways. But Jo's tryin' to change that."

"How?"

"Teachin' the youngin's about their ancestors.
Makin' 'em proud of bein' Scotch-Irish."

"Who will assume your responsibilities one day?"

"Don't rightly know. Katie's showin' a bit of interest
in my healin' herbs."

Katie? The six-year-old? Did Granny believe she'd
live long enough to hand down to the child the medical
knowledge necessary to care for the clan? Maggie questioned whether her grandmother would even be able to
travel by horseback much longer. She had trouble en-
visioning Granny plowing through high snowdrifts and
blizzard conditions to help those in need. "How do you
get around during the winter months?"

"When I was a mite younger, I'd ride through the snow, but my bones don't like the cold no more. A lot of folks got telephones these days. They get a hold of Jo and she goes out 'n brings 'em to my cabin if'n they can't come on their own."

"Wouldn't it be easier to build a facility that was accessible by car?"

"The clan ain't got that kind of money."

What made Granny believe she was an expert on the costs associated with running a clinic? She doubted the old woman had a savings account. As a matter of fact she wondered if her grandmother even knew who the president of the United Sates was.

Maggie, that was mean.

Ashamed that she'd allowed her frustration to get the best of her, she volunteered, "I'm sure federal funds and organizations exist that would help."

"We don't want no flatlanders—I mean, outsiders—comin' up here tellin' us what we gotta do." Granny's standard response to everything.

"But the clan members are entitled to the best medical care possible."

"Ya sayin' I can't care for my people?"

She hadn't meant to insult her grandmother. "No, Granny. I'm sure you do your best. But what about the times your herbs or medicines aren't enough? When the sick or injured require a prescription medication to fight illnesses or infections? What about X-ray machines for broken bones, and a lab to perform simple blood and urine tests?"

"Don't need no machine to figure out what's ailin' folks."

Maggie disagreed but kept silent. No sense arguing

with the stubborn woman. Besides, her grandmother's doctoring wasn't any of Maggie's business and the clan wasn't her responsibility. Easy to say, but the nurse in her, who had modern medical technology to diagnose patients daily, rebelled.

Lost in contemplation, Maggie wasn't aware they'd arrived at their destination until Blue snorted and stopped in front of a rickety old shack that made Granny's cabin look like a fancy bed-and-breakfast retreat. A narrow porch ran the length of the wooden structure. Big chunks of mortar were missing from between the logs and rusted sheets of tin had been nailed over the roof.

Granny slid off Raison and flung the reins around the porch post, then grabbed her medical satchel and climbed the steps.

"Jeb," she hollered. "It's Granny. Ya decent? I'm a comin' in." Without giving the man an opportunity to answer, she stomped inside, leaving Maggie to figure out how to get off Blue.

Hoping to increase the circulation in her numb rump, Maggie wiggled in the saddle. A tingling sensation ran the length of her left leg as she lifted her foot free of the stirrup. With concerted effort, she managed to drag her leg over the horse and slide to the ground. As soon as both feet hit dirt, her legs buckled and she clutched the saddle horn for balance.

Groaning, she rested her cheek against Blue's sweaty hide until the million tiny pinpricks tormenting her thighs and buttocks receded.

When she faced the cabin, a pack of hound dogs, tails wagging, waited on the porch. She wobbled up the steps, patted each dog on the head, then hovered in the doorway, her eyes adjusting to the dim interior.

The cabin was dank and musty, and a hint of dog urine lingered in the air. The ashes in the fireplace were cold. Flies buzzed around empty food cans piled on the kitchen table. A large bag of dog food had tipped over and spilled out. The hounds must have had a fine old time—only a few scattered nuggets remained on the floor.

"Why you still in bed, ol' man?" Granny clucked at the figure lying on a cot shoved into the far corner. She cracked the window above the bed, creating a cross breeze through the cabin.

Maggie welcomed the fresh air and moved farther into the room. The place needed a maid and a good scrubbing. Muddy paw prints decorated the wood floor, creating a pattern of sorts. No curtains hung on the windows. No frilly doilies sat on the tables. Not one sign of a female presence anywhere.

"Does Jeb live alone?" Maggie asked in a hushed voice.

"Jeb's a widower. Just him and the dogs now."

The animals had remained in the doorway. Poor things were probably tired of the smells inside, too. "How is he?" Maggie crossed the room and paused at Granny's side.

"Powerful hot." Arthritic hands tested the whiskered cheeks.

When Maggie checked his brow, the heat pouring off his skin hinted at a temperature of 102. *Infection*—a reasonable deduction, seeing as how Granny probably hadn't given him any antibiotics after she'd stitched the wound.

Jeb moaned in his sleep and Granny shushed him, then unwrapped the bandage on his hand. Maggie winced at the jagged cut across his palm. Red, swollen and oozing yellow puss. "How did this happen?"

"Sharpenin' his huntin' knife."

"What did you wash the wound with?"

"Scrubbed it real good with hot water and lye soap. Then I doused it with witch hazel." Granny rested Jeb's arm across his stomach and checked the pots on the table, sniffing the contents of each. "Made two teas— sweet angelica, to fight infection, and goldenseal." Hands on her hips, she muttered, "Stupid fool. He ain't drank any of it."

"He's going to require an antibiotic to beat this infection. Where's the nearest hospital?" Maggie asked.

Ignoring the question, Granny griped, "I'll fix more of the tea 'n pour it down his gullet until he chokes."

"The stitches should come out and the cut cleaned again, Granny."

For a moment, her grandmother appeared ready to argue, then she sighed, "I'll git my scissors. Ya boil the water."

Working together, Maggie and her grandmother cleaned the infected area, gave Jeb a sponge bath and changed the linens on the cot. By then, the wound had stopped oozing enough to suture it. Granny lit a match and stuck the needle in the flame, then fed the thread that had been soaked in witch hazel through the eye of the needle.

"Impressive," Maggie said, complimenting her grandmother's sutures. She'd never witnessed a surgeon's hands put in a stitch as straight and as tight as Granny's arthritic fingers had managed.

"Pass me the kit," Granny commanded. "Got me a salve inside." While she rummaged through the contents, Maggie cleaned the mess they'd made. She glanced at the doorway, having forgotten about the dogs. The mutts slept on the porch, except for the biggest, who'd remained at the door. "What's his name?"

"That there's Beauregard. He's Jeb's favorite."

The old man grumbled a protest and Maggie rushed to his bedside, where Granny massaged a cream over the reddened skin. Eyes fluttered open. He stared in confusion, then sputtered and attempted to sit up.

Granny planted a palm in the middle of his chest and shoved him against the mattress. "Don't get yer Irish up, ya old coot."

"Water," he croaked.

"Got some tea fer ya." Granny held the tin cup to his mouth. He grimaced but swallowed the liquid, then closed his eyes and drifted off again.

"He really should go to a doctor." Maggie worried her lower lip as she studied the wounded hand, which had ballooned to twice the size of the other. At least no red streaks ran up his arm—yet.

"Give the tea time to work 'afore ya go spoutin' off that yer Granny ain't got a lick o' sense."

Ignoring her grandmother's hurtful jab, Maggie asked, "Where do we take him if needs more help than you're able to give?"

"Finnegan's Stand."

"But I thought they didn't have a medical clinic."

"They don't. The rescue squad comes from Slatterton and picks up folks at Scooter's Café."

"How far is Slatterton?"

"'Bout an hour."

The hollow should have a clinic closer than an hour

away. Noticing Granny's drooping posture, Maggie didn't have the heart to begin another argument over the need for proper health care in the hollow. Instead she settled in a chair by the kitchen table. "Should we help him to the outhouse?" There was no toilet in the one-room cabin.

"He ain't gonna want a young girl catchin' him buck naked."

"How will you manage if he's unsteady on his feet?"

"He's not gonna pee fer a spell." Granny flashed Maggie an irritated frown. "Not till I git more tea in him."

"We can't leave him alone."

"'Course we can't."

Maggie was afraid to ask. "Then we're sleeping here tonight?"

"I'm stayin'. Yer headin' to Tom's place. I'll be home tomorrow or the next day."

She glanced at the empty shelves on the wall. "What about food for you and Jeb?" Maggie didn't approve of her grandmother staying by herself. There was no bell to ring if trouble broke out.

Granny must have read her mind, because she insisted, "I'll be fine. Got me fruit and nuts in my bag. Don't eat much more 'n that."

"How will I find my way home?" Maggie corrected herself. "I mean, to your cabin."

"Blue'll git ya there."

"You expect me to trust a horse to navigate these woods?"

"Blue's been walking this mountain all his life. He won't get lost."

Granny puttered with the covers across Jeb's chest,

and Maggie suspected her grandmother had a soft spot for the geezer. She considered how alone her grandmother was. The woman had lost her daughter years ago, then her husband. Yes, Granny had friends in the clan, but that wasn't the same as having family around. What a shame Maggie's mother had never found the courage to confront her parents and attempt to reconcile. All their lives would have turned out quite different—not necessarily better, but different.

"I'll be back tomorrow to check on the two of you." Maggie headed for the door. "Should I bring anything besides a few groceries?"

"More of this here tea."

"What about them?" Maggie nodded at the hounds.

"They'll hunt up a squirrel fer supper."

Eeew. "Until tomorrow then." Maggie stepped over the dogs and approached the horse. After delivering Blue to his owner, she intended to drive to the Moorelands' cabin and use their telephone. She worried that without antibiotics Jeb wouldn't beat the infection. Going behind her grandmother's back didn't sit well with Maggie, but saving Jeb's hand was worth any verbal lashing the old woman might let loose.

She glared at Blue. "Don't even think of misbehaving, buddy." Her thigh muscles protested at the prospect of climbing onto the gelding. Discomfort aside, what if the horse followed a wrong turn and she became lost? Weeks might pass before a search party located her.

Chicken.

Hey, a city girl had a right to be nervous. Shoving aside her trepidation, she approached Blue and rubbed his belly. "Be a good boy. Take me home and I'll make sure your papa offers you a nice big carrot." She grasped the reins, swallowed a moan and shoved her foot into the stirrup. Ignoring the twinge in her rump, she clicked her tongue. "Home, Blue."

The gelding trotted through the clearing, then slowed when he picked up the trail. They'd traveled less than thirty minutes before the horse tensed. Swiveling her head, Maggie searched the woods but noticed nothing amiss. A moment later, a *thwack* rent the air and Blue bolted.

Her squawk was cut short when the horse switched directions and almost unseated her. Grasping his mane, she bent low and clung. Blue zigzagged through the dense foliage, causing Maggie to slide so much out of the saddle that she was hanging off one side of the horse. After what felt like forever, the gelding burst into an open field. Maggie managed to peek over Blue's rump and realized he was headed full speed toward… *Abram?*

"Watch out!" she screamed.

In the nick of time, Abram jumped out of the way as the gelding sped past. Maggie heard Abram holler her name, but she was too focused on keeping herself from falling off and being trampled to respond.

"Whoa, Blue!" Her high-pitched command appeared to excite the horse and he picked up momentum. The muscles in Maggie's arms burned and she prayed for the strength to hang on until Blue exhausted himself. Fifty yards later the horse slowed to a trot and then a walk, and then stopped and reared. Maggie released her grip and fell to the ground with a *thud,* knocking the wind from her. She rolled out from under Blue's hooves, then lay on the ground gasping for breath.

"Maggie!"

Abram.

"Maggie! Answer me! Where are you?"

She crawled to her knees, but when she attempted to stand, her wobbly legs folded and she collapsed. Abram's yelling made Blue nervous, and the animal stomped the ground, his sides heaving.

"Bad boy," Maggie wheezed.

By the time Abram broke through the underbrush in true commando form, Maggie's lungs hadn't relaxed enough to take a much needed deep breath. Light-headed from lack of oxygen, she attempted to reassure Abram, but couldn't find her voice. Her heart turned to mush at the concerned expression on his face. When she made another attempt to stand, he ordered, "Don't move."

In his rush to reach her side, his limp was more pronounced. If he was in any pain, he didn't let on. He dropped to his knees. "Are you hurt?"

Maggie noticed that the lower portion of his leg bent at an awkward angle, and she worried that he was causing himself more discomfort. "I think so," she squeaked.

He ran his big, callused hands along her limbs and around her ankles, his strong fingers pressing deep, checking for fractures. Then he touched her shoulders, and she couldn't prevent a shiver from racking her body.

"Did that hurt?" His gaze cut to her face as he examined her collarbone, his fingers sliding beneath the material of her T-shirt.

Abram's touch rattled her as no other man's ever had. She stared into his brown eyes, urging him to understand that the only thing that hurt her right now was the yearning for his kiss.

ABRAM WILLED HIS RACING heart to calm as he checked Maggie's arms, discovering only a couple of scratches—thank God. The fear that had surged through him when she'd raced by on the horse was like none he'd ever experienced—which told him he cared way too much about Maggie. More than was good for his well-being.

"Hold still." Embarrassed by the shaky note in his voice, he threaded his fingers through her thick hair, searching her skull for lumps and bumps. He found softness and heat. Relieved she wasn't injured, he released the air caught in his lungs. *Big mistake.* Just as at the racetrack, her scent went straight to his head. Maggie O'Neil was slipping further and further past his defenses. He couldn't let himself need her. Anxiety mixed with fear clawed its way up his throat and he demanded, "What are you doing on a horse when it's obvious you don't know how to ride one?" He winced at Maggie's round-eyed expression. He hadn't meant to be harsh…just to push her back over to her side of the boundary line. In a calmer voice, he added, "You might have been killed."

Without a word Maggie got to her knees. Abram offered a hand up but she swatted his fingers out of the way. *Stubborn woman.* A trait she no doubt inherited from her grandmother.

"I'm sorry I scared you." She took one step and groaned.

"What's wrong?" He wrapped an arm around her waist, ready to catch her if she lost her balance. Her warm body—mainly a breast—rubbing against his chest messed with his concentration and he momentarily forgot the question on his mind. She grunted when she attempted another step and he asked, "Sprained ankle?"

"Sprained butt," she muttered, limping toward the horse.

Torn, Abram assisted Maggie to the animal. Ever since the stock-car race yesterday, he couldn't get her out of his head. He didn't want her to leave, yet he didn't want her to stay. Without a word, he cupped his hands and offered her a boost. She bit her lower lip as she swung a leg over the saddle. Damn, she was a tough lady. He was beginning to believe there wasn't much about Maggie that didn't impress him.

"To answer your earlier question, I'm riding Blue because Granny and I were checking on a patient this morning. Granny decided to stay the night to keep an eye on him and I was instructed to deliver the horse to the clan blacksmith."

And if the horse rebelled again? The next time, Maggie might not be so lucky. And he wouldn't be around to help. "I'll follow you."

"That's not necessary. Blue knows the way."

"Leave the horse at my cabin and I'll drive you back in the Jeep." He didn't care for the idea of Maggie riding alone through the woods.

"We'll be fine." She grabbed the reins and Blue moved forward.

Abram wanted to say something, anything, to keep her with him longer. At the edge of the clearing, she called over her shoulder, "Why are you always chopping wood?"

Like a cold bucket of water, the question doused any fantasy he harbored that he and Maggie might—

What? Have a relationship? Disgusted with himself for desiring things he had no right to, he turned his back on her and walked off.

Chapter Six

Sweat beaded Abram's brow as he hunched behind the bushes outside Granny O'Neil's cabin. He'd had plenty of experience spying in the military, but this was the first time he'd stumbled upon a woman preparing her bath. Etiquette dictated he scram, but no one had ever accused him of possessing manners.

The late-afternoon sun dipped low in the sky, its rays bouncing off the back porch, making Maggie's image hazy at best. She dumped another bucket of water into the tub, then stripped off her clothes. If he was a gentleman—which he was not—he would walk away, but he was powerless against the urge to peek at her feminine curves. He swallowed his disappointment when only her silhouette remained visible. She dipped a big toe into the water, then eased into the tub.

All afternoon, Abram had debated his rude behavior with Maggie. She was entitled to his apology. In the end his conscience had gotten the best of him and he'd driven to Granny's cabin, hoping she'd accept his invitation to Scooter's Café and allow him the chance to make amends.

Admittedly, saying "I'm sorry" was the last thing on

his mind right now. Although he hadn't been able to view the details of Maggie's body, knowing she was naked beneath the water was enough to arouse him—a condition he hadn't experienced often since leaving Iraq.

The war had changed him. He wasn't the same soldier as he'd been when he'd first set foot in the Middle Eastern country. No longer was he able to discount his feelings—Maggie tested his emotional control as no other.

She was beautiful. Vibrant. And he didn't want to ignore her. For the first time since quitting the army, he wished to lose himself in something other than misery. To immerse himself in Maggie if only for a short while.

According to his watch, twenty minutes had passed since she'd rested her head against the edge of the tub. Had she fallen asleep? Stealthily he approached the porch. Maggie didn't move, which confirmed his earlier suspicion. She was snoozing. Or else—heaven forbid—she'd drowned while he'd been arguing with himself in the bushes. He paused at the bottom step, then grinned as the sound of Maggie's snores reached his ears.

Leaning a shoulder against the doorjamb, he made himself comfortable. An odd tightness squeezed his chest as he listened to the breathy sounds coming from her mouth. She appeared peaceful, almost angelic. He wondered if nightmares of patients she'd been unable to help ever plagued her sleep. Patients who'd died because she'd made the wrong diagnosis.

He failed to recall the last time he'd slept straight through the night until morning without nightmares jarring him awake. Would he ever close his eyes and *not* see the faces of wounded women, children, innocent bystanders and soldiers? And why did the nightmares always begin after he slipped into a deep sleep, where he should be most at peace?

Because you don't deserve peace.

For Maggie's sake, he hoped she never experienced anything close to the horrific night terrors that tormented him. Little by little they ripped him open and flayed his soul. Maggie was too beautiful, too good to suffer such torture.

"You're lucky I don't haul a shotgun around like my grandmother." The muttered threat carried through the screen door.

Abram jerked upright. Maggie's eyes were closed. Had he imagined her voice?

"When it comes to perverts, I shoot first, then ask questions." One green eye cracked a slit. "How long have you been ogling me in my bath?"

"Not long," he assured her, relieved she didn't appear upset by his presence. "You were so peaceful I didn't want to disturb you."

Snort. "What do you want?"

She might not be throwing a tantrum, but she wasn't tossing out the welcome mat, either. "I came to say I'm sorry."

Both eyes opened fully. "Soldiers don't apologize."

True. But…"I'm not a soldier anymore."

"Once a soldier, always a soldier." She examined her fingertips. "I'm shriveling."

He'd settle for a shriveled version of Maggie any day. "I was rude this afternoon and I—"

"It's none of my business why you chop wood." She

wrinkled her nose. "For all I care, you can cut down the entire Appalachian forest."

The I-don't-give-a-damn attitude didn't fool Abram. Maggie cared. That knowledge alone had prompted him to seek her out.

"The physical activity is therapeutic." There. He'd offered an explanation.

"Therapeutic as in physical exercise or therapeutic as in an anger management exercise?"

Tell her. She's a nurse, not a bimbo who will believe anything you say. "The second one."

"You're suffering from post-traumatic stress disorder." It wasn't a question but a statement.

"Cut right to the chase, don't you?"

"I'm a health-care professional. What did you expect?"

Told you so. His struggle with PTSD was private and, if he had his way, would remain private. "Have you eaten?"

"Why?" One raven eyebrow arched. "Do you expect me to cook for you?"

Little spitfire. "I was hoping you'd join me for supper at Scooter's Café."

"Are you buying?"

He grinned. "Yep."

"Okay, I'm in." She grabbed the sides of the washtub. "Don't look."

He spun, putting his back to the screen door. The sound of splashing water sent his imagination into overdrive as he conjured an image of Maggie naked and wet.

"Give me ten minutes," she said, then went inside.

He meandered to the front yard of the cabin, where

he'd parked the Jeep. A short while later Maggie
appeared, wearing a pair of khaki shorts and a burnt-
orange tank top under a beige V-neck sweater. Forcing
his gaze from her toned legs and the fantasy they
inspired—mainly how the limbs would feel wrapped
around his waist—he got the Jeep door for her. As she
slipped past him, he breathed deeply, then coughed
when a medicinal smell shot up his nostrils.

"Sorry about that," she said. "I added eucalyptus to
the bathwater."

"What for?" He waited to shut the door until she
got situated.

"To ease sore muscles."

No doubt the muscles she referred to were south of
her waistline. He'd offer to massage her fanny but
figured she'd pass. When he'd driven to the end of
Granny's dirt trail, he asked, "Any news on the car?"

"No. I expect to hear something by Friday."

Maggie didn't elaborate, which led Abram to
wonder what her agenda was *after* Friday. Did she plan
to remain in the area or head to Louisville? Part of him
wished he and Maggie would have more time together
before they said goodbye—forever. After a stretch of
silence, he realized she didn't intend to carry the conversation. Her quietness disturbed him—surprising for
a man who'd hadn't been bothered by three years of
eating one hot meal in a twenty-four-hour period,
wearing an unwashed uniform weeks on end and using
a hole in the ground for a toilet.

On a good day Abram wasn't much of a talker and
his men had preferred to keep their own company when
they went off duty. He'd felt the same way. Maintain-
ing an upbeat attitude when inside he questioned

whether there would ever be an end to people killing people on earth hadn't been easy. As commander he'd prided himself on offering an open-door policy, wherever that might be—cot, trailer or the hard ground. He'd allowed his men to talk, scream or cry on his shoulder if they needed to. Better his men crumbled in front of him than the enemy.

Often, the soldiers had retreated inside themselves to relive the day's patrol while jamming to their favorite tunes on their iPods. Hell, he hadn't blamed them. His soldiers had been fresh-out-of-high-school kids from every corner of America. Listening to music had provided the one activity during the day that they'd shared with their counterparts back home. Abram hadn't had the heart to interrupt them with adrenaline-pumped speeches about upcoming patrols. Half the time he'd been too damn tired to sleep, let alone to conduct pep rallies.

Even so, Abram had been available to his men 24–7. A few had sought him for advice on how to handle problems with their girlfriends. War did a number on a soldier's psyche. Many young men had feared their significant others were two-timing them. Odds were the young ladies would cheat, but Abram had never suggested as much. Instead he'd spouted a bunch of bullshit about how a woman loved a man in uniform, until his charge would strut off like a rooster. Then the Dear John letter would arrive and he and the soldier would begin the whole cheer-John-up process again.

"Are you thinking about the war?" Maggie motioned to Abram's hands.

Embarrassed that she'd caught him choking the steering wheel, he relaxed his grip. "What was wrong with Granny's patient?"

"That wasn't very subtle," she accused.

"I prefer not to talk about my stint in the military." He held his breath, hoping she wouldn't press him.

"The patient's name is Jeb. He's around Granny's age."

Abram exhaled, relieved Maggie had agreed to respect his privacy. "What happened to him?"

"He cut his hand sharpening a hunting knife."

"Will he be okay?"

"Granny thinks her homemade remedies work miracles. I'm worried that the infection will worsen without the help of an antibiotic."

"Why hasn't he gone to the hospital?"

"Answering that question would lead to a conversation on the stubbornness of certain people in this area. I'd rather not get into it right now." Her vivid green eyes glittered with agitation, hinting at an Irish temper. He could easily imagine drowning in her gaze during love-making.

"Scooter's is known for its country-fried steak and burgers," he blurted, forcing his mind from the gutter.

"Oh, goody. More healthy food," she grumbled.

Abram parked in front of the café. "As they say, 'When in Rome…'"

When they walked through the door, Betty Sue spotted them and pointed to a table in the far corner. Once they were seated, the waitress showed up with water glasses.

"Today's special is country-fried steak with sawmill gravy." Betty Sue waited expectantly.

"Sounds good." Abram handed his menu to the waitress.

Maggie pursed her lips. "Where are the salads?"

Betty Sue frowned. "We serve real food."

"Make that two specials then." After the waitress slipped away, Maggie whispered, "Is she always that friendly?"

Abram grinned.

"You're smiling," she pointed out.

"I do that on occasion." Her bubbly laughter knocked him off balance—in a good way. Being with Maggie made him feel lighter, cleaner inside than he'd felt in a long time.

"Tell me about your family," she coaxed him, then sipped from her water glass.

Mesmerized by the movement of her throat when she swallowed, he managed to say, "I'm the youngest of six kids."

"Wow, big family. I was an only child."

"My mother was forty-five when she had me. By the time I entered high school my brothers and sister had all married and had their own families. My parents are dead now."

"Are you close to your siblings?"

"Not anymore. After graduating from college, I joined the military and spent the years living everywhere but Ohio."

"What was your major in college?"

"Accounting."

Her eyes widened. "I wouldn't have guessed you were a numbers man."

"Math came easy for me. A degree in accounting seemed logical. But when graduation rolled around, I'd decided I wanted some adventure before I worked nine-to-five every day." His turn to ask the questions. "You getting along with your grandmother?"

"When I first arrived in the hollow, I'd intended to gather my mother's belongings and then be on my way." She shrugged. "Now I'm…confused."

"About what?"

"Who I am."

How did he respond to a statement like that?

"I grew up believing my grandparents were these horrible people who didn't love my mother and didn't care that she'd run away and now… Well, Granny cried when I explained my mother's fight with cancer. I think in her own way she really loved her daughter, and missed her terribly through the years."

"Sorry about your mother," he offered, suspecting Maggie had been tight with her parent. Abram hadn't been warm with his folks. It wasn't that he hadn't liked them. He just hadn't *known* them. His siblings had raised him because both his father and mother had worked.

"Maybe my mother was partly to blame for the strained relationship with her parents." A silky strand of hair fell across Maggie's eye and Abram resisted the urge to tuck it behind her ear.

"Has your grandmother shared any details of your mother's life in the hollow?" His curiosity surprised him, then he decided he'd asked the question because the sound of Maggie's voice soothed him.

"I'm afraid to bring up my mother. When I mention that Finnegan's Stand should have its own health clinic, Granny flies off the handle."

"Rural people respect one another's privacy. They don't appreciate strangers encroaching on their territory. I've been here a little over a month and most locals avoid me." He didn't confess he preferred it that way.

"Privacy is one thing, but what happens when a family member or neighbor requires the kind of medical care my grandmother can't provide? What about children? Prenatal checkups for pregnant mothers? Childhood vaccinations? People need access to modern medicine."

Although he sympathized with Maggie's point of view, Abram had been on the receiving end of too much help after returning from Iraq, and he'd reached a limit where he hadn't wanted doctors or therapists to mess with him anymore. But he was an adult, not a child, and he'd been willing to pay the consequences of walking away from rehab before he'd completed his treatment program.

Betty Sue delivered their food, poured Abram's coffee, then promised to check back in a few minutes.

Maggie scowled at her plate.

"What's the matter?" he asked.

"Trying to decide which of my main arteries is going to shut down after this meal." She stabbed a piece of breaded okra. "Even the vegetables are deep-fried."

"Trust me. The food's worth an artery. Maybe two." He shoveled a forkful of fried apples into his mouth.

Grimacing, Maggie scraped the white gravy off the top of her steak, then painstakingly cut away the breaded coating. After eating three pieces of meat, he teased, "Not bad, huh?"

Mouth full, she nodded. He was halfway through his meal by the time she'd finished the steak and dived into the okra and fried apples.

"When was the last time you ate anything?" he asked.

"Breakfast. And that was skillet ham with gravy."

They finished their meal in silence, both scraping their plates clean. Betty Sue cleared the table, refilled his coffee and left a dessert menu.

"Peach cobbler's good," he suggested.

"Would you order that for me?" Maggie stood. "I have to make a phone call to a coworker."

As soon as she stepped outside, Abram waved Betty Sue over. "We'll both have the peach cobbler."

"Meal okay?" The waitress paused at their table.

"There isn't a bad meal anywhere on the menu, Betty Sue."

She motioned to the front window. "Everything okay between that gal and Granny?"

Abram rolled his shoulders. He hated gossip. He'd been the recipient of stares, whispers and comments when he'd arrived here after leaving Iraq. If Betty Sue wanted details, she'd have to pester Maggie for them.

"Seems decent, but she'll never fit in." Clearly not interested in striking up a friendship with Granny's granddaughter, Betty Sue didn't stick around when Maggie reentered the café.

"Good news," Maggie announced, taking her seat.

"Yeah?"

"A nurse I work with has agreed to overnight a few medical supplies and an antibiotic for Jeb."

"Doesn't a doctor have to prescribe the medicine?"

"I'm licensed to dispense medication, but a doctor at the clinic has to review and sign off on my patient charts every sixty days. I'll fill out the paperwork on Jeb when I get back to Louisville and make it official."

"So you're sneaking behind Granny's back?" he teased.

"Yes." She quirked an eyebrow, daring him to comment.

That Maggie stood up for what she believed in was admirable, but Abram anticipated she'd have a hell of a fight on her hands when the old woman discovered what her granddaughter had done.

"Granny's teas won't fix Jeb's hand. It's not that I'm against holistic healing—" Maggie continued when Abram remained silent "—I'm not familiar enough with her remedies to judge them. But I've observed modern medicine work. Jeb needs a strong antibiotic or he'll become septic. If the infection is left untreated, he may lose his hand or worse, his life."

Dessert arrived and Abram realized that he hadn't followed through with his reason for inviting Maggie to supper. Before he sampled the cobbler, he apologized. "I'm sorry about this afternoon. I should have answered your question instead of walking away."

"Apology accepted."

That was a breeze.

Maggie sampled her dessert. "Delicious." They ate in silence, then she pushed her empty plate away. "Thank you for dinner."

After tossing a five-dollar bill on the table, he grabbed the check Betty Sue had left when she'd delivered the cobblers. While he waited in line at the register, it occurred to him that he'd worried for nothing over inviting Maggie to supper. He'd expected the meal to be tense and the conversation stilted. But like their afternoon in Pikesville, he'd found her company enjoyable and relaxing, which made ending the evening and heading to his cabin—alone—all the more difficult.

They drove to Granny's in silence. The sun had set

thirty minutes earlier and the mountains prepared for sleep—a luxury Abram did without most nights. If he was fortunate, he'd catch a few catnaps, which lasted twenty or thirty minutes. He glanced at Maggie, who sat with her head against the seat, eyes closed. He imagined sleeping with her body curled against his side, her soft scent masking the odors of war and death that permeated his nightmares.

As soon as he swung onto the potholed drive that led to Granny's cabin, Maggie awoke. He parked. "I'll walk you to the door." By the time he moved around the hood of the Jeep, Maggie had already let herself out. He reached around to shut the door, and his fingers accidentally brushed her fanny as she moved out of the way. He fisted his hands to keep from swinging her around and… *What? Kissing her?*

Yes, he yearned to sample her sexy mouth. But one taste wouldn't quench his thirst. He'd want more. And he couldn't take that risk with Maggie. At the front door they stood awkwardly in silence, their gazes skimming each other's faces but never making eye contact.

Thank her for a nice evening and leave.

Not until he kissed her. But God help him, he wanted her to make the first move.

She did. Standing on tiptoe, she aimed her lips for his cheek. At the last second, he angled his head and their mouths collided. He tensed, expecting her to pull away—she didn't. Gathering his courage, he relaxed, angled his head and closed his eyes.

Her lips softened beneath his as he increased the pressure. With a tenderness he would never have expected himself capable of, he kissed Maggie. The experience was better—way better—than he'd dreamed. Beautiful, innocent, arousing, her mouth seduced him.

A sigh of pleasure escaped her and he resisted the urge to move her hips closer. His arousal escalated until he had a full-blown hard-on. Why now? Why Maggie? Ending the kiss, he whispered, "'Night, Maggie," and walked off into the dark, frustrated…full of yearning—

"Abram, wait!"

He froze with his hand on the Jeep's door handle. Maggie rushed over to him. He waited for her to speak, but she seemed content simply to stare at his mouth.

"Kiss me again," she murmured.

This time he slid his fingers through her hair, tilted her head and angled his mouth. Slow and gentle he covered her lips. He wanted more, so he nibbled the corner of her mouth, then licked the tender spot, nuzzling her soft cheek. Swallowing a groan, he begged with his tongue for entrance. Her mouth was cool and moist and tasted like peaches. He couldn't get enough of her.

At some point during their kiss she wrapped her arms around his waist, went up on tiptoe and rubbed her breasts against his chest. The groan he'd swallowed previously worked its way back up his throat and rumbled from his mouth. He wasn't sure how, but she'd managed to back him up against the Jeep door and plaster herself against him. He dropped his hands from her hair and clutched her hips, bringing her in contact with his arousal. This time Maggie groaned.

Tongues played. Hands searched. Mouths clung.

Their kiss had become a full-fledged make-out session. He wished nothing more than to lay Maggie down and love her, but he didn't dare—because giving her up after having her would be next to impossible.

Eventually they had to breathe, and their mouths broke apart. He rested his forehead against hers while he gathered the strength to leave. Realizing that Granny wasn't home and that Maggie probably wouldn't object if he accompanied her inside made saying goodbye excruciating.

Gathering the last of his strength, he walked to the driver's-side door and hopped into the Jeep. As he drove off, he checked the rear-view mirror. Maggie watched him, her fingertips pressed to her mouth.

Please, God, let me dream about her tonight.

Chapter Seven

Cock-a-doodle-do!

Maggie bolted upright in bed, her head woozy with visions of Abram kissing her. In fact, Abram's face had materialized on and off in her dreams throughout the night. She rolled over in her grandmother's heather-scented bed, shoved her head under the pillow and forced her thoughts back to the way Abram's mouth had caressed her lips and his—

Cock-a-doodle-do!

Blasted rooster.

So much for fantasizing about Abram's mouth before heading into Finnegan's Stand to await delivery of the antibiotic for Jeb. She sat up and rubbed the sleep from her eyes. In the still-dark room, Maggie wasn't sure if the sun had risen or not. After stumbling into the main living area, she pulled aside the curtain across the front window. A luminous haze greeted her.

Once she'd dressed in a T-shirt and running shorts, Maggie grabbed the afghan off the back of Granny's rocker, slipped into a pair of flip-flops and left the cabin. Breathing deeply the crisp morning smell— damp earth, piney forest and decaying vegetation mixed with a hint of heather, she tiptoed across the yard to the rocking chair beneath the maple tree. She sat down in the rocker, drew her knees up, wrapped the afghan around her and shivered at the dewy coolness.

Cock-a-doodle-do!

Maggie studied the surrounding woods but spotted no sign of the rude bird. The nuisance must belong to a neighbor of Granny's. She gazed heavenward, and the same as the previous night when she'd rested her head on the pillow, Abram's face popped into her mind.

Lord, the man was handsome, and now she intended to add good kisser to the list of his traits that appealed to her. No doubt about it, Maggie was attracted to the solider. Abram hadn't gone into detail about his PTSD, but if his chopping wood was any indication, he had a serious case of the disorder. As a nurse she possessed a general understanding of PTSD but had never dealt with the condition firsthand.

She often contemplated how a woman said goodbye to one man and hello to another when her soldier returned from war.

In Maggie's case, she hadn't met Abram before he'd enlisted in the military. The man she knew was the one who chopped wood for hours and preferred to be left alone—or so he claimed. That he'd asked her out to eat suggested he yearned to connect with another human being.

She compared being around Abram to working a jigsaw puzzle. She could spend days, weeks, months fitting the pieces of him together, only to discover his deepest, darkest secrets were missing, leaving the puzzle incomplete.

Thinking back on her search for doctors and treatments that might have saved her mother, Maggie wondered if reaching out to Abram would have the same results—that in the end nothing she did would make any difference. Did she have the strength to survive that kind of pain again?

You act as if you and Abram are already committed to each other.

Committed—no. But Maggie was kidding herself if she didn't 'fess up that Abram stirred her. He'd stood in front of her, nervous, waiting for a sign that she wanted him to kiss her. Bestowed the barest touch of his lips…allowing her the opportunity to change her mind. She hadn't been prepared for such consideration. His hesitancy had made her yearn for him all the more.

Now in the light of day, she admitted she was a tad embarrassed that she'd run after him and begged for a second kiss. As soon as their mouths had met though, she'd decided that she'd pay any price for Abram's caress. He made her feel cherished and desired—all things she hadn't felt in so, so long.

Always a sucker for the underdog, she pursued him. Maggie anticipated losing her heart to Abram. Her need to care for others made her a great nurse but put her in a vulnerable position with the opposite sex.

Instinct insisted it had been a long while since Abram had been involved in a relationship. How many women had he had in the past? Had he been dating anyone special before he'd shipped off to Iraq?

Good grief. How had a couple of kisses led to all this overanalyzing, which served only to make her head throb? She was nuts if she expected anything serious to develop between them. Her life was in Louisville and Abram's was here in the mountains. Depending on what the dealership said about the car tomorrow, she might depart from the hollow as soon as Saturday. In light of that, she decided to stop agonizing about the future. She'd enjoy Abram's company until it was time for her to head home. After checking in with Granny and Jeb later today, she'd invite Abram on a picnic—an innocent, harmless picnic between friends.

"'BOUT TIME ya showed up." Granny stood on Jeb's porch, arms crossed over her chest, mouth all but swallowed up by the wrinkled folds of her face. As far as greetings went, Maggie had received worse from uncooperative patients.

"I had to pick up a delivery in town this morning." She slid off Blue and patted the gelding's rump, then tied the reins to the porch rail. Today he'd behaved like a good boy. "I brought a few groceries for Jeb and lunch for you." She motioned to the cloth bundle tied to the saddle. "How's Jeb doing?" she added when her grandmother continued to glare.

"He ain't gettin' better."

Maggie hurried up the steps. "What happened?"

Granny's hunched shoulders straightened and her chin lifted. "Nothin' happened. He jest ain't coolin' off."

She followed her grandmother into the cabin, then went straight to Jeb's cot and placed a hand against his forehead. "He's burning up."

"Couldn't get no more tea in 'im after midnight." Granny hovered, wringing her hands.

That bothered Maggie. If the old man had trouble swallowing or opening his jaw, he might have tetanus from the cut. "Is Jeb up to date on his tetanus shot?"

"Can't say," Granny answered.

"I brought along fluids, and an antibiotic." Maggie left the cabin and retrieved the box of medical supplies secured to Blue's saddle. Back inside, Granny pressed wet rags to Jeb's face and neck in an attempt to cool him off.

Maggie unpacked two bags of a lactated Ringer's solution, which contained electrolyte fluids—potassium, sodium, chloride and calcium and penicillin G—the IV form of the antibiotic. With luck Jeb wouldn't require all four doses, but he'd need at least two. While she fiddled with the collapsible IV stand, she ignored Granny's narrow-eyed glances. When she approached the cot with an alcohol wipe, she anticipated an argument. Instead Granny surprised her and moved out of the way.

After cleaning Jeb's uninjured hand, she hooked up the IV. Once she adjusted the drip set, she inserted a second tube to administer the antibiotics and explained, "The Ringer's solution will help Jeb stay hydrated while he battles the fever." Motioning to the small bag, she added, "That's a medicine to fight infection." Maggie was pleased her grandmother paid attention. "He'll have to have at least two of those bags in him before signs of the infection will abate."

"If the infection don't clear up?" Granny asked.

"Then we transport him to a hospital."

"Where'd ya get all that fancy equipment?"

"From the clinic I work at in Louisville."

Nothing more was said as Maggie retrieved the stethoscope, blood pressure cuff and ear thermometer from the supply box. She took Jeb's vitals. "His temp's 103. Blood pressure's a bit high—140 over 90." She listened to his chest. "Lungs are clear." Granny's eagle eyes observed Maggie's every move. For someone who claimed not to believe in modern medicine, her grandmother sure was nosy. "How old is Jeb?" she asked.

"Eighty-somethin'."

"Is he on any medication for high blood pressure?" Evidently not, judging by her grandmother's perplexed expression.

"Sit, Granny." Exhaustion ringed the old woman's eyes. She probably hadn't slept all night. "You should eat."

"Don't go fussin' over me," she protested, but did as Maggie requested. Jeb's dog Beauregard moved next to Granny's chair.

While Maggie unpacked the sandwich and fruit salad she'd purchased at the café in town, she noticed Granny's hand stray to the dog's head. Buried under seventy-seven years of stubborn pride was a touch of sweetness. "Enjoy." Maggie placed the food on the table, then searched the kitchen area for a dog-food bowl. She ended up using a plastic food-storage container and filled it with the dry dog food she'd picked up at the gas station convenience store. As soon as she set the bowl on the porch, the rest of the pack came bounding out of the woods, tails wagging.

"Ain't ya eatin'?" Granny asked.

"I'll eat a little later." Maggie shifted her chair toward Jeb's cot so she could monitor the IV.

When Granny finished her meal, she pushed the plate away, then grumbled, "Thought I done told ya to keep away from that soldier."

"What are you talking about?"

"Heard ya was at the café with 'im."

Irked by the tone of disapproval in Granny's voice,

Maggie snapped, "Who I choose to have dinner with is no one's business but my own." Good grief, had her grandmother sent someone to spy on her?

"Everythin' in this here holler's my business."

Maggie opened her mouth to argue but remained silent when her grandmother held up a hand. "I ain't gonna let it happen again."

Maybe Granny had acted this way when her mother had dated Maggie's father. "Let what happen?"

"Ain't gonna have another one of my girls sneakin' off with a no-good skunk hunter."

Skunk hunter? Maggie didn't know whether to laugh, scream or cry. She appreciated that Granny cared enough to worry about her, but rebelled against the old woman's belief that she had a right to dictate Maggie's actions.

"First of all, I am not one of your girls." Maggie might be related to Granny, but as far as any *family feelings,* the two were still more acquaintances than relatives. Maggie got up to check the IV. "Abram is a nice man. He minds his own business and doesn't bother anyone."

"He ain't one of the clan."

Facing her grandmother, Maggie stated, "And neither am I."

"Yer mama thought she was better'n us, too. Didn't do nothin' fer her but get her dead."

The cruel remark cut deep and Maggie swallowed a gasp. Why would the old woman say such a thing about her own daughter? *Because she's hurting, Maggie.* Was the shimmer in Granny's eyes the result of anger or sorrow? Hard to tell. Before Maggie muttered something she'd regret, she took Jeb's vitals again

and switched out the bag of Ringer's lactate. She waited
a few more minutes, then replaced the antibiotic with
a new bag. "He should be fine for a while," Maggie announced, and strode from the cabin.

Granny didn't put up a fuss. Not that Maggie had
expected her to. If her grandmother hadn't run after her
daughter all those years ago, why would she chase after
her granddaughter now? Fighting tears, she hopped on
Blue and rode toward Abram's cabin.

ABRAM STOOD AT THE cabin window. Fifty yards from the
front door, partially hidden in the woods, Maggie sat
astride the same horse she'd fallen off of yesterday. She'd
been lingering for almost fifteen minutes, but had yet to
announce her presence. He had no idea what had brought
her here today… Well, maybe he had one idea. Their kiss
last night. It had been the best and worst mistake he'd
made in a long time. Best, because her kiss had made him
feel like a man again. Worst, because her mouth had made
him wish for things that could never be. He and Maggie
might be attracted to each other, but they had no future.

He'd been sitting on the end of his bed, sorting
through fishing tackle, trying to come up with a reasonable excuse to see Maggie again, when he'd heard the
whinny of a horse. Immediately his mind had conjured
up an image of the green-eyed Maggie.

Was she here to say goodbye? He didn't want any
goodbyes. And he sure as heck didn't trust himself not
to beg her to stay. *Go home, Maggie.*

As if she'd read his mind and decided to ignore his
plea, she got off the horse, grabbed the reins and led the
animal out of the woods, into the clearing in front of the
cabin.

His eyes drank her in. She wore white athletic shoes, jeans that ended mid calf and a neon-pink T-shirt with writing on the front. Her hair was braided into two long ropes on either side of her head, and for a second he pictured her strolling the mountains wearing a doeskin dress and moccasins. She would have made a breathtaking Indian princess.

He yearned to speak with her, to just be with her, yet at the same time he acknowledged that the more time he spent with her, the more difficult watching her walk away would be. Nevertheless, the closer Maggie got to the cabin, the more his belief that kissing her had been a big mistake and his vow to keep his distance failed to make sense.

As she strode farther into the yard, her gaze shifted to the chopping stump and the ax leaning against the wood. Was she recalling the afternoon she and the little girl had spied on him? After wrapping the reins around the lower branch of the tree at the corner of the cabin, she retrieved the cloth bundle tied to the saddle, then climbed the porch steps.

Three knocks.

Like a man walking to the gallows, he dragged his feet across the room and opened the door. She greeted him with a smile, and the sparkle in her eyes stole his breath. "In the mood for a picnic?" she asked.

For an instant, logic reared its ugly head and he grappled for an excuse to refuse Maggie's invitation. But the chance to lie with her on a blanket in the shade was like a dream. "I'll grab the drinks." Why not waste a couple of hours with her when she was as good as gone in a few days. Besides, what the hell else did he have to do today—chop more wood?

After fetching two cans of pop from the fridge he stepped onto the porch. "The property has a pond." He moved past her and went to the horse. "Blue might as well tag along and get a drink."

Maggie fell in step with him, their arms brushing as he led the horse into the woods behind the cabin. Wishing he had the nerve to ask why she'd waited before knocking on the door, he settled for, "How's the patient doing?"

"I hope Jeb will show signs of improvement by the time I return to check on him. I administered fluids and an antibiotic."

"Did Granny put up a fight?"

"No. She realizes how serious Jeb's condition is."

"How old is your grandmother?" Abram's foot twisted and he lost his balance, careening into Maggie and knocking her sideways. "Damn, I'm sorry."

"No problem." Her smile eased his embarrassment. Half the time he stumbled around like an idiot. "Granny's in her late seventies."

"What happens when she won't be able to help others any longer?"

"I suppose someone will fill her shoes."

When Maggie didn't elaborate, he said, "Interesting coincidence that you and your grandmother share a love for medicine."

"Don't think I haven't considered that. Drives me crazy."

"What's wrong with having that in common?" He veered south, motioning to a break in the trees.

"She's the last person I'd ever want to be like." The odd note in Maggie's declaration made Abram believe she hoped to convince herself that she and her grandmother weren't alike.

They walked in silence until they emerged from the woods into a small oasis with a spring-fed pond. A carpet of thick green grass and patches of yellow and pink wildflowers surrounded the water.

"This place is beautiful." Maggie set her bundle on the ground and approached the water's edge. Abram gave Blue a drink, then hitched the gelding to a fallen log where he had plenty of fresh grass to eat. By the time Abram collapsed to the blanket spread over the ground, Maggie had removed her shoes and socks and stood ankle deep at the edge of the pond.

"Join me. It's nice and cool." She bent at the waist and splashed a handful of water in his direction.

Her playful demeanor brought a smile to his face, and he reached to remove his shoe. His hand froze on the laces. Nonchalantly he straightened. "You go ahead. I'm starving." He removed a sandwich from the sack and pretended interest in the food while he observed Maggie. She waded through the water toward the horse, speaking in soft tones to the animal. A short while later, she joined him and accepted the can of pop he held out.

"Thanks." She guzzled the drink. "You said someone gave you this land."

"The property belonged to the family of a soldier under my command. Eric Monroe. His parents live in the St. Louis area."

"What happened to Eric?" she inquired.

"He died in Iraq."

"I'm sorry, Abram. I can't imagine losing a friend under such circumstances."

Hell. He still had trouble accepting that the bright, good-looking, determined-to-trounce-the-terrorists soldier was dead. "He turned twenty-two the day before he died." *What a frickin' waste.*

"And his parents no longer visit here?"

"Not since Eric was killed. Too many memories."

"How long do you plan to stay?" Her eyes twinkled when she teased, "Until you run out of trees to chop?"

Smarty-pants. He grinned. "Probably." He offered her a sandwich. "Thanks for bringing lunch."

After she took a bite, he asked, "What about you? In a hurry to get back to Louisville?"

One finely arched eyebrow lifted. "What you really want to know is whether there's a man waiting for me at home."

Okay, so the thought had crossed his mind a time… or two…or three.

Lips curving, she whispered, "I wouldn't have allowed you to kiss me last night if I was involved with someone."

At Maggie's admission, relief flooded Abram. How easily he could get caught up in fantasizing about a future with her.

"What about you?" She nudged his shoulder. "Women love soldiers."

Whole soldiers, not mangled ones. "I had a steady relationship in college. We broke up when I joined the army. After that, I never stayed in the States long enough to become serious with a woman."

Maggie's hand edged toward his face and he tensed, then grunted when she smacked his forehead. "Sorry." She wiggled her fingertip with a smashed bug on the end. "Gnat."

"I've had worse crawling on me. Next time let the poor creature live." His gut clenched at her laughter.

Conversation ceased while Maggie finished her

meal, and he surreptitiously studied her profile. He decided that he'd never met a woman with such a stubborn tilt to her chin—or such a beautiful face. They had more commonalities than he'd anticipate. Not in appearance—no one would call *his* face attractive. Surprisingly, neither of them was in a relationship. For all intents and purposes they were alone in the world—he, having cut ties with his family years ago and she, having lost her mother. *But now she has her grandmother...* "Have you thought about sticking around Heather's Hollow permanently?"

"And doing what?" Maggie stuffed the sandwich wrapper inside the sack, then passed him a chocolate-chip cookie.

"Considering Jeb's injury, I'd say there's a need for a qualified nurse in the area."

"I have no desire to trespass on my grandmother's sacred healing grounds." She wrinkled her nose. "The clan isn't ready for the upheaval that would result in a clash between old world ideas and modern medicine. I'd end up arguing with my grandmother daily." She swept her hand in front of her. "But these mountains...call to me." She cast him a sheepish glance. "Sounds stupid, doesn't it?"

"Not at all." He tugged her braid until he had her attention. "The mountains have a way of making a person feel safe." This was the first place he'd found after his tour in Iraq that he'd believed the war was unable to touch him. Physically, that is. Mentally, the war had penetrated every pore of his body. Now he questioned if it was Maggie who made him feel safe and the mountains were just an illusion.

"I'm in awe my mother grew up here."

"Why did she run off?"

"She claimed my grandparents had shunned her after they'd discovered she'd gotten pregnant."

"I'd say your mother did fine raising a daughter like you without her family's help. You're a credit to your mother's memory."

"Thanks." She stroked his cheek and Abram clenched his jaw in reaction to her gentle touch. "Mom and I were close. After my father died, it was the two of us until the end. Her death made me aware of how alone I was—am—in the world. I guess I'd hoped that by making the trip to Heather's Hollow I'd discover that my grandmother wasn't the cold woman my mother had made her out to be all those years."

He pried. "And is she?"

"The jury is still out." Maggie picked a pink wild-flower and twirled the stem between her fingertips. "Sometimes I believe Granny did love my mother. But I sense she resented her at times. I wish I knew the truth about what happened between them."

"Why don't you ask?"

Reclining on the blanket, Maggie studied the sky. "I'm afraid to hear the truth."

He could relate. More often than not, the truth hurt. Careful to keep several inches of space between their bodies, he joined her in sky gazing.

"Enough about me and Granny. What are your plans for this land?" She rolled her head sideways, her breath puffing against his chin.

Crap. He should have figured he'd pay a price for being nosy. He didn't want to tell her his idea of building a hunting lodge because he wasn't certain that was what he really intended to do. "I'm not sure."

"How long have you been out of the army?"

"Six months." Technically. He'd checked out long before he'd arrived for rehab at Walter Reed Army Medical Center in Washington, D.C.

"I suppose you're not eager to find an accounting job."

"Are you dissing my degree?" he joked, and was rewarded with her sweet laughter. After years of military service, sitting at a desk from eight to five would be torture. Although using his brain cells once in a while might force his mind to conjure up dreams of numbers instead of the same old bloody nightmares.

An exasperated sigh escaped Maggie. "Half of me yearns to cut and run from this place, and the other half wishes to stick around and force my stubborn grandmother to acknowledge that the hollow deserves a medical clinic."

"Why not stay and see what develops between you two?" *And between you and me.*

"I can think of one plus if I remain longer."

He swallowed hard. "What's that?"

In a move that took him by surprise, Maggie nudged her breasts against his arm. "You."

Heart thumping, he murmured, "Me, huh?" When she smiled, he was tempted to tweak her braids.

"Yeah, you."

Kiss me, Maggie.

She must have read his mind, because she brushed her lips across his. He opened his mouth and deepened the kiss. Needing to taste her, he cupped the back of her head and held her steady as he thrust his tongue inside her mouth and explored her sweetness. Their sighs became moans.

Arousal hit him, swift and hot. That Maggie could wring such an intense response from him brought both relief and terror. Relief that his male parts appeared in working order after malfunctioning since his injury in Iraq and terror that he might not be all Maggie hoped. He wanted her badly—almost as badly as he wanted to be whole again. Careful to disguise his lust, he shifted away, but she followed, not ready to break their embrace.

"Touch me," she commanded.

Where?

Grabbing his hand, she flattened it to her right breast. He massaged the soft mound, debating whether to replace his hand with his mouth. A taste. A sample of what could never be his.

Ah, Maggie. You should have left well enough alone. But she didn't. She inserted her leg between his thighs and crawled on top of him. When her shoe clunked against his left boot, Abram's hot lust turned ice-cold. His reaction was automatic. He bolted upright, unseating her. "I'm sorry," he gasped.

Face red with embarrassment, Maggie mumbled, "I didn't mean to get carried away." She attempted to stand, but he snagged her arm and she froze, refusing to make eye contact with him.

Abram battled the urge to erase her discomfort, but doing so meant confiding in her. Not a chance. He didn't care to view her face when she learned the truth about his disability. Years from now when he pictured Maggie in his mind, he'd remember how she'd gazed at him moments ago—with heated desire. "It has nothing to do with you. It's…" he bumbled.

"Nothing to do with me. Right." She scrambled to

her feet and began gathering the picnic supplies. Abram had little choice but to get off the blanket, lest she bundle him up inside it.

He yearned to keep Maggie with him in their quiet little glen where the outside world ceased to exist, yet at the same time he wanted her gone so he wouldn't have to explain what had happened in Iraq. Maggie would demand details. And Abram didn't have the guts to confess the entire truth—especially how he'd failed his men. He didn't dare try to stop her when she untied Blue and hopped on. A click of her tongue and the horse trotted off. He waited for a goodbye…

Nothing. No wave. Not even a glance in his direction.

Now, *that* was more along the lines of what he deserved.

Chapter Eight

The pages of Granny's medicinal journal blurred before Maggie's eyes as her mind strayed to Abram—again. She struggled to understand what she'd done or said that had caused him to abruptly push her away during their impromptu picnic. He'd acted as if she'd groped him like a hussy instead of offering a simple kiss. And darn it, he'd kissed her with as much fervor as she'd kissed him.

Maggie had assumed Abram was as attracted to her as she was to him, especially after their good-night kiss following dinner at the café. Had she imagined the heat in his gaze that evening? Or maybe Abram was erecting walls to protect himself from becoming involved with her, since she intended to leave the hollow—

Knock, knock, knock.

The pounding brought Maggie's musings to an abrupt end. Setting Granny's journal aside, she uncurled from the rocking chair and answered the door. The man on the stoop smiled, and for a split second her heart stalled before she recognized the visitor had blondish-brown hair, not dark brown like Abram's. Heart resuming a normal beat, she said, "Hello."

"I'm Sullivan Mooreland. My wife creamed your car last weekend."

Smiling, she shook the hand he offered. The man looked exactly as Katie had described her father during their hike through the woods a few days ago—tall and slim, with a pit in his cheek. "Maggie O'Neil. Nice to meet you."

Once inside the cabin, he studied her with such intensity that Maggie wiped her mouth, wondering if she had crumbs on her lips from the sandwich she'd eaten at lunch. "Jo's right," he announced.

"About what?"

"You have Granny's green eyes but your black hair—" He moved sideways several feet, so that from his vantage point, the sun streamed through on her. "Ah. There it is."

"There what is?"

"Red highlights."

"Huh?"

"You don't have the bright red hair that many of the clan members sport, but you're Scotch-Irish." He glanced around the cabin. "Is Granny here?"

"She stayed the night at Jeb's."

"How's his hand healing?"

"Better. Would you care for some iced tea?"

"Sounds great." He followed her to the kitchen area and took a seat at the table.

"Yesterday I administered a round of fluids and anti-biotics that brought his fever down. I plan to check on him this evening." Maggie poured the tea into her grandmother's Mason jars and delivered them to the table.

"Jo said you were a nurse."

"Nurse-practitioner. I specialize in family medicine."

"Lucky for Jeb you happened to be visiting."

Maggie grimaced. "Not according to my grandmother."

Eyes twinkling, Sullivan teased, "A bit old-fashioned, is she?"

"That's putting it nicely." After a lull in the conversation, Maggie inquired, "What brings you by?"

"Two things." He removed a piece of paper from his shirt pocket and handed it to her. "The dealership phoned the house this morning with an official list of the repairs and the costs."

"Did they say when the car would be ready?" Maggie knew nothing about automobiles and had no clue what the noted repairs entailed. When Sullivan remained quiet, Maggie glanced up, and winced at his frown. "How long?"

"Two weeks. They said the damage was more extensive than they'd first thought."

Drat. What was she going to do? She had more vacation time due her, but hadn't planned on using a year's worth all at once. She could hop a bus back to Louisville and retrieve her car when it was ready. Neither option appealed to her, however.

"By the way…" Sullivan stood, then fished his wallet from his pants pocket. "Jo and I are paying the deductible." He set five one-hundred-dollar bills on the table.

"How did you—"

"I asked the manager at the dealership."

"Please, I can't—"

"Jo won't have it any other way. Besides, I'd like to sleep in my own bed tonight." At her perplexed expression, he added, "My wife threatened to lock me in the cookhouse if you refused the money."

"Cookhouse?"

"Long story."

Laughing, she said, "You're not part of the clan, are you?"

"I lived in Seattle, Washington, before I drove out here this past spring to cover a story for the *Seattle Courier.*"

"You're a journalist?"

"I freelance now. Anyway, the story I was after turned into more than I'd bargained for."

"Really?"

"Ever heard of Lightning Jack, the notorious Appalachian bootlegger?"

She shook her head. Maggie's mother had never spoken the name.

"Lightning Jack was Jo's grandfather. After he died, Jo took over his still and continued to brew and sell moonshine to his customers."

Fascinating. "His buyers didn't care that Lightning Jack wasn't making the whiskey?"

"No one *knew* he'd died. For years the clan elders had kept it secret that Jo's grandfather and Lighting Jack were one and the same."

"Why?"

"Selling moonshine is illegal, but Jo needed the money to fund her school in the hollow."

"Katie mentioned that her mother was a teacher."

"Jo led me on a wild-goose chase, hoping I'd give up and go back to Seattle." He grinned. "I might have— if I hadn't fallen in love with her." His smile faded. "Love doesn't guarantee everything will be smooth sailing. On some issues Jo and I remain worlds apart."

"I understand. Granny doesn't trust modern medicine."

"Exactly." He slapped his hand on the table. "Jo and I went around in circles over a lot of things, but in the end all that matters is our love."

"So you left your life in Seattle and moved to the hollow?"

"It wasn't much of a life."

"Mind if I ask how you're earning a living now?"

"Jo and I are collaborating on a book about the clan and Appalachian culture. We snagged an agent with our proposal, and he's found a couple of interested publishers. When I'm not writing on the book, I sell articles to various magazines and journals."

"Glad things worked out for you two, but I don't picture that happening with me and Granny."

"She'll come around in time," he assured her.

"I doubt it." Maggie snorted. "When I asked why the hollow or Finnegan's Stand didn't have a medical clinic, she bit off my head."

"Granny's admitted to Jo that she's concerned about who will follow in her footsteps as clan healer."

"Don't look at me that way." Maggie squirmed. "I have no intention of moving here and becoming a backwoods healer. Besides, I don't belong here."

He chuckled. "Don't be too sure."

"Doesn't matter what anyone believes. Granny doesn't approve of modern medicine. In her opinion, anything that grows in a petri dish and doesn't spring from the ground is poison."

"She allowed you to treat Jeb's hand," Sullivan pointed out.

"Thank goodness for that. The old man escaped losing his hand or worse, dying from a blood infection."

"Granny can be intimidating. She didn't approve of my presence in the hollow for the longest time."

"I suppose she tried to run you off with that shotgun she carries everywhere with her."

He nodded. "She stole my clothes while I was bathing and I had to sit and chat with her in nothing but a towel until Jo rescued me."

Oh, good grief.

When Sullivan walked to the door, Maggie said, "Thank you for bringing news about my car. I'll have to discuss my vacation schedule with my supervisor and see what I can arrange."

"You're welcome to stop by anytime to use the phone or just visit." He snapped his fingers. "Almost forgot the second reason for my visit. Jo's throwing a surprise seventy-eighth birthday party for Granny this Sunday afternoon at our place. You'll be here to bring her over, won't you?"

Why not? This might be the only time Maggie celebrated her grandmother's birthday. "When do you want us?"

"Noon." Sullivan paused on the stoop. "Speaking of moonshine…ever taste heather whiskey?"

"Can't say that I have."

"Jo's brewing a special batch for the celebration. It'll knock you clean on your keester."

"I'd prefer to keep my *keester* off the ground, but I'll try a sip."

"Catch you Sunday." With a wave he hopped into a snazzy red Corvette and drove off.

"C'MON, GRANNY," Maggie coaxed for the third time in as many minutes.

"Ain't hungry," the old woman grumped.

Maggie had suggested they eat lunch at the café today. On the way, she planned to switch directions and drive to Jo and Sullivan's for the surprise birthday gathering. She hadn't counted on her grandmother's stubbornness, or the hurt feeling Maggie had squelched when Granny had failed to announce that today, September fifteenth, was her birthday—as if she didn't care for her grand-daughter to know.

"A quick lunch. I promise."

"I'm headin' over to Jeb's."

"We visited him last night. He's fine." But Granny seemed to believe he'd relapse, or that the antibiotics Maggie had administered would stop working. Granny refused to acknowledge what was right before her eyes—that Jeb's hand was healing. His fever had broken, the infection had disappeared and he'd been out of bed, moving around yesterday.

For all her efforts, Maggie had received nothing more than a nod of thanks from her grandmother. Granny had snubbed Maggie's attempt to explain the consequences of not properly treating infections. Jeb, on the other hand, had appeared fascinated by her medical equipment and had even asked to listen to his hounds' heartbeats with the stethoscope.

Instead of being thrilled that Jeb's hand had been saved, her grandmother had behaved as if Maggie's skill and knowledge threatened her position as clan healer. Maybe Maggie was overanalyzing the situation. Her grandmother's dark mood might simply stem from the fact that she didn't appreciate turning another year older.

"We'll see Jeb soon." That was the truth. Jo had

promised Maggie that Sullivan would bring the geezer to the party.

Shoulders slumped in defeat, Granny tugged her shawl from the rocking chair and shuffled to the door, which Maggie had held open the past five minutes. Granny's sullenness had Maggie debating whether to take the additional two weeks of vacation her supervisor had approved yesterday.

When Maggie had informed Granny she wanted to remain in the hollow until the Honda had been repaired, she'd hoped for a small sign of pleasure from the old woman. A smile or maybe, "That's nice, we'll have time to become better acquainted." After all, Granny had promised to teach her about the uses of heather. Instead Maggie had received a sour pout and a "Suit yerself." Renting a car and driving home to Louisville had tempted her, but then Abram's face had flashed through her mind and Maggie had decided to put up with her cantankerous grandmother in order to be around Abram a little longer.

Something in Abram drew Maggie. Although he wasn't fighting in Iraq anymore, the enemy had followed him home. She yearned for him to confide in her and to allow her to assist him with whatever he was struggling with. Even though he'd admitted to suffering from PTSD, Maggie perceived there was more to Abram's grief than tormenting nightmares. She admired his resolve to spare others from the effects of his condition. He was the kind of man who would suffer in silence to protect others. If he'd agree to it, Maggie could be the shoulder he leaned on.

Be careful, Maggie. You might end up giving him more than your shoulder. Maybe your heart. Then where will you be?

The desire to be with Abram occupied most of Maggie's thoughts. If only she wasn't so attracted to the man. The soldier was a heartache waiting to happen, and Maggie was vulnerable right now. She'd lost her mother recently enough that being alone in the world scared her. Granny might never be family.

Maggie's fascination with the soldier aside, her instinctual urge to heal his invisible wounds wouldn't permit her to desert him.

What if he doesn't want your help?

She wouldn't accept no for an answer.

Because Granny insisted on driving, Maggie lied, "I forgot. We're stopping at Jo's so I can call my insurance agent."

Grunting unintelligibly, her grandmother drove in the opposite direction of Finnegan's Stand. "What in tarnation's goin' on here?" she complained, almost sideswiping a parked car along the road leading to the Moorelands' cabin.

Keeping a straight face, Maggie remained quiet.

When Granny parked at the end of the driveway, a group crowded around the truck and shouted, "Surprise!"

Maggie broke out laughing at her grandmother's grimace. She'd done her part and delivered the guest of honor; now the others would have to tease the birthday girl into a better mood.

With an arm around Granny's frail shoulders, Jo escorted her across the yard and seated her in a rocking chair decorated with streamers and balloons. Several gift-wrapped boxes sat on the ground, and Maggie cringed—it hadn't even occurred to her to buy her grandmother a birthday gift. Then Jeb approached the chair and Maggie decided she'd saved Granny's friend's life—that was better than a store-bought gift.

Forgetting her worry, Maggie meandered through the crowd, greeting people she'd never met, attempting to act as if she didn't feel out of place. Stares burned her back as she stood in front of the refreshment table and served herself a glass of punch.

"You cost me a dollar I didn't have to give away, Maggie O'Neil."

Holding back a smile, Maggie faced Annie McKee. "How did I cost you a dollar?"

"I bet my boys—" the younger woman pointed across the yard to two teens wrestling by a crumbling stone structure. "—that you'd never get Granny to the party."

"Sorry," Maggie apologized. She motioned to the boys. "Twins?"

"Bobby and Tommy." Annie's maternal smile was filled with love for her sons. "Double trouble, but they're worth it." Right then a man swaggered over and joined them. Although the afternoon was still young, he appeared to have had too much… What had Sullivan called it? Moonshine. "Sean, this here is Maggie O'Neil, Granny's granddaughter."

The man's eyes narrowed as he sipped from a small jug. "Didn't know the old woman had any kin." Annie tensed at her husband's less-than-friendly greeting.

"My grandmother wasn't aware I existed until a few months ago." Maggie had to hope Granny had at least wondered about the child her daughter had been pregnant with, whether her daughter had given birth to a boy or a girl. When an uncomfortable silence settled upon the group, Maggie announced, "I'm from Louisville. I work as a nurse-practitioner in a hospital clinic."

"Takin' after Granny." Sean wiped a hand across his mouth.

"The skills I use in caring for my patients aren't quite the same as Granny's healing methods." As soon as Maggie uttered the defensive statement, she wanted to yank it back. She refused to debate the merits of holistic healing versus modern medicine—not when there was little chance of winning over this crowd. "What do you do for a living, Sean?" she asked, changing the subject. According to the pained expression on Annie's face, Maggie's effort was not appreciated.

"I worked at the sawmill, but the wife wasn't happy with the money I made, so now I'm bustin' my ass in the Blue Coal Mine." He threw an arm around Annie's shoulder and flashed a sardonic grin. "Ain't that right, darlin'?"

Annie's expression remained impassive, although Maggie swore steam rose from her short-cropped carrot-colored hair. "I want my boys to go to college."

"No, what you mean is you don't want the boys turnin' out like their old man." Sean squeezed Annie's shoulder until she glared.

"I better go mingle," Maggie said, then walked off to join the group of men congregating near the front porch. Tom Kavenagh met her at the bottom step. "Come to sample a bit o' moonshine, Maggie?" he asked.

She eyed the jug in his hand. Had it been passed around, each man chugging from the opening? As if he'd read her mind, Tom answered her, "Just opened this here jug."

Still...

After pouring an inch of amber liquid in a plastic cup, he held it out to her.

"That's barely a swallow."

"A swallow's all a gal yer size can handle."

Maggie wasn't much of a drinker, but she'd tossed back a few shots with her nursing classmates during college. She swallowed the contents in one gulp, then promptly clutched her throat. Tears poured from her eyes and she gasped for breath.

Good God, I'm going to die from asphyxiation while a bunch of men guffaw in my face. Then Sullivan was there, patting her shoulders and whispering, "Next time try the spiked punch. The stuff these guys drink is ninety proof."

Ninety proof? Was that legal? *Don't ask.* Stomach on fire, she wheezed, "Thanks, but I'm done drinking for the day."

All of a sudden Sullivan's smile disappeared and his gaze darkened. He focused on something over Maggie's shoulder and the men's raucous laughter ended abruptly. She shifted her watery gaze to the far end of the yard and spotted Abram at the trailhead. Eyes darting from one person to the next, he acted as if he'd stumbled into the enemy camp instead of a birthday party.

"Hey, Miss Maggie, look!" Katie pointed to Abram. "It's the stranger we spied on in the woods."

Oh, boy. Now their secret was out in the open. Katie's declaration sent Sullivan stalking across the ground. Maggie set her cup on the step and followed, with Katie right on her heels. Abram's gaze connected with Maggie's and her chest squeezed at the message in his brown eyes—*I shouldn't have come.*

"Katie Mooreland, have you met this man?" Jo joined the gathering at the edge of the yard.

"Miss Maggie and I watched him chop wood," the little girl answered.

"I didn't extend you an invitation to the party. Who are you?" Sullivan demanded.

Before Abram had the opportunity to answer, Maggie began the introductions. "Sullivan, I'd like you to meet Abram Devane. He lives in the cabin behind Granny's property."

Jo's husband didn't offer his hand. "That doesn't explain how my daughter knows him," he growled.

By now Granny had shuffled over. She squinted at Abram.

"Katie and I were out hiking through the woods the other day and we stumbled upon Mr. Devane's cabin." Maggie opted to exclude details of Katie's previous visit alone, believing it would only complicate the situation and put Abram in a worse light.

"Mr. Abram likes to chop wood, don't you?" Katie smiled.

A red hue seeped across Abram's cheeks. "Betty Sue at the café in town mentioned that Mrs. O'Neil was celebrating her birthday today and I thought the party would be a good opportunity to introduce myself to neighbors." He switched his attention to Granny. "Happy birthday, ma'am."

"How long ya plannin' to stick round these parts?" Granny demanded, not impressed with the soldier's birthday sentiment.

Abram's gaze slid to Maggie. "For a while."

"Katie, you leave Mr. Devane alone, you hear? I don't want you anywhere near him or his property," Sullivan warned the child.

"Sullivan," Maggie protested, "Abram would never harm Katie and—"

"He's a stranger," Jo interrupted. "We can't trust him."

Anger rattled Maggie, and she blurted, "He's perfectly safe. I can see him. I mean, I sense things…oh, never mind," she bumbled.

"*See* as in he told you he wouldn't harm Katie?" Jo glanced at Granny. "Or see as in here." She touched a fingertip to her temple.

Maggie's mouth sagged. Was it possible that…

"Go on, Granddaughter. Explain how ya know this man means Katie no harm."

"Sometimes I have these powerful feelings about people. I can sense their intentions." She turned to Abram. Where had he gone? Her gaze flew down the trail leading into the woods, and she caught sight of his blue T-shirt a second before the bushes swallowed him whole. Facing the group gathering around her, she continued. "Abram would never hurt Katie."

Jo placed a hand on Granny's shoulder. "You have your answer now."

"What answer?" Maggie asked.

"You inherited the sight from Granny, Maggie," Jo said.

"Is it true? Do you see things, too?"

Granny nodded, and something akin to relief surged through Maggie. All these years she'd believed she was a freak, when she wasn't. "Mom never mentioned that you—"

"Skips a generation." Granny's face went gray, and she grumbled, "Where's my rocker," before strolling off to the chair.

Apparently Granny didn't appreciate sharing the

limelight with anyone—not even her own flesh and blood.

Jo smiled. "I think it's wonderful that you'll be able to assume your grandmother's duties one day."

Oh, no. Maggie was a nurse, not a *healer* or an *elder.* She refused to change the way she practiced health care—not even for the clan. Not even to earn her grandmother's acceptance or respect.

Before she said something she'd regret, Maggie fled in search of Abram.

Chapter Nine

"Abram! Wait up!"

Damn. Abram stopped midstride, ending his retreat into the woods behind the Mooreland cabin. He didn't want Maggie to trip and knock herself out chasing after him.

He'd hoped to make a clean getaway from the birthday party and cursed himself for showing up in the first place. When Betty Sue had mentioned the celebration, he'd engaged in a mental debate until he'd arrived at an excuse to attend the party that had nothing to do with Maggie—to introduce himself to the clan and get a feel for their reaction to his idea of building a hunting lodge in their backyard.

Five minutes among the locals and he'd had his answer without even broaching the subject. The cool glances and suspicious stares cast his way convinced him that he, and anything associated with him, wasn't welcome in the hollow. That alone wouldn't have been enough to send him on the lam, but add the shock of learning Maggie possessed some sort of uncanny ability to see inside people and he couldn't escape fast enough.

Abram had traveled the globe throughout his military career and he'd been exposed to exotic cultures whose members highly regarded a person's supernatural or mystical gift. Who was he to doubt Maggie's ability to *know* certain things about people?

What if she'd *seen* more of him than he'd intended for her to see? Like, how much he desired her? How much he admired her? How hard he was falling for her?

And what about his disability? Had she pictured that in her head? Too bad if she had, because he refused to grant her an up-close-and-personal view of his leg. *No way.* What a mess. He'd planned to spend as much time with Maggie as possible until she left for Louisville. Now if they were together, he'd wonder if she was reading his mind.

"Hey." Maggie stopped a few feet away, bent at the waist and gulped in air. "Why'd…you…run…off like that?" Her hair was windblown; her cheeks pink from running. He yearned to pull her into his arms and kiss her. *Careful, Abram. She might be reading your thoughts right now.* He retreated a step, hoping distance would bar Maggie from his mind. "I wasn't welcome."

Shaking her head, she insisted, "You're wrong. Once I explained—"

"When I walked into the yard," he interrupted, "the clan appeared ready to sever my head with their bare hands."

Maggie wrinkled her nose. "You don't have to be so graphic."

"Once a soldier, always a soldier," he reminded her. "Graphic is— Was my life for twelve years." He didn't usually expose his crude side to civilians, but he'd make an exception in Maggie's case. Maybe if she got a glimpse of the darkness inside him, she'd run and save them both a lot of heartache.

"The clan is suspicious of everyone. As soon as I explained who you were—"

"You mean, once you told everyone you could *see* who I was."

Her gaze slid away from his face, confirming what he'd feared—she understood a lot more than she let on.

"It's not what you think," she protested. "I'm not some kind of voodoo madam or seer. I don't gaze at crystal balls or read tarot cards."

"Then what are you, Maggie?" He studied her face, searching for a sign of truth in her declaration.

"Sometimes I sense things about people. It's not something I can control and it doesn't happen with everyone I meet."

"Guess that makes me special then." He regretted the sarcastic words when Maggie's eyes rounded, but too much had happened in his lifetime to make him monitor his speech. "What kinds of things do you sense?" he asked, extending an olive branch

"Pain. Hurt. I can guess if someone is lying to me."

Abram winced. "What do you see when you look at me?"

"My ability doesn't turn on and off like a light switch."

"When we first met outside the café, I remember you staring at my face."

She nodded. "Because you're handsome."

He swallowed hard. "Anything else?" The lengthy silence that followed his question tied Abram's gut in knots.

"I noticed your limp when you crossed the street."

Sweat beaded along his brow. "And…?"

"I thought you might have suffered a war wound or possibly a sport's injury."

"That's all?"

"My nursing background picked up on your PTSD."

Aside from her guessing correctly about his struggle with PTSD, she couldn't *see* what happened in Iraq. If he had his way, she never would. "You're positive that's it?"

"Yes. Why? Are you hiding something?"

You have no idea. And he damn sure wasn't allowing Maggie the opportunity to get close enough to risk her viewing the horror he lived with because of one bad judgment call. "You better go back to the party." Before he took a step, she had his shirt sleeve in her grasp.

"Abram, what's wrong?" When he would have protested, she added, "If I've upset you…"

"No." He pulled his arm free and steeled himself against the hurt in her eyes.

"Probably best now if we keep our distance from each other." Her gasp sliced through his chest, but he forced the words out of his mouth. "Besides, you'll be leaving as soon as your car is ready."

"And our friendship?"

Friendship—is that what she considered their kisses and touches? "Maggie, you're a nice—"

"Save the Dear John speech." She propped her fists on her hips and glared. "Don't patronize me by letting me down easy. If you don't want anything more to do with me, then say so."

Abram appreciated her fighting spirit, but better to end their relationship now than later. Her attraction to him was evident in her touch, her words, her kisses, even in the way she studied him—like now, with those bottom-less green eyes. And her gorgeous eyes were the very reason he intended to say goodbye. He'd courageously faced the enemy and had survived battles, IEDs and mortar attacks. But deep in his gut he doubted his strength would hold in the face of Maggie's horror when she discovered the seriousness of his disability and the grave mistake he'd committed that had cost his men's lives.

Time to focus on the future. The real future—not the fantasy future he'd dreamed of having with Maggie. "I'm closing up the cabin and leaving the hollow. I don't know when I'll be back." It wasn't a lie. He'd been toying with the idea of approaching one of his former superior officers with a business proposition. Retired Colonel Bellwood was an avid outdoorsman from Indiana. Abram intended to pay the colonel a visit and discuss his hunting-lodge idea. He anticipated the army officer would give a few pointers on dealing with the locals and their animosity toward outsiders. And if all worked out as planned, Maggie would be long gone by the time he returned from Indiana. "Take care, Maggie." He shoved his way through the dense under-brush, his ears burning with the silence that trailed him.

TAKE CARE, MAGGIE...

Maggie believed her ability to sense things about people had caused Abram to panic. Seven long and lonely days had passed since he'd announced he was leaving.

Feeling sorry for herself, she sat on the stone bench in the center of the heather labyrinth on her grand-mother's property. Her car would be ready around the end of the month—eight days from now. She wondered if Abram would show up before she left for Louisville.

Had Abram's standoffishness the afternoon of Granny's birthday party been caused by the cold-shoulder reception from the clan or by the fact that Maggie's *gift* was out in the open between them? She suspected the latter. What was Abram hiding from her? Was it something so terrible that he wouldn't risk being with her because he feared she'd sense the truth?

If Granny had noticed Maggie's moping, the old woman hadn't commented. Her grandmother had been wallowing in her own blue funk since the party. What a pair they made, pouting in silence.

The swoosh of birds taking flight from the trees alerted Maggie to another's presence in the labyrinth. Granny trudged along the path, shoulders slumped, appearing every one of her seventy-eight years. When she reached the bench, Maggie scooted aside.

They sat for a time before Maggie spoke. "Who built this labyrinth?"

"Yer mama and I did most of the work."

"Mom helped you?" Maggie would have never guessed her mother had been interested in such a folk-loric activity.

Granny's weathered face relaxed and the corners of her mouth tilted in a semblance of a smile. "Yer mama and I never argued till she met that…yer daddy."

Sadness filled Maggie at the idea of her mother and Granny growing so far apart that they were unable to make amends before it was too late.

After swatting at the fly buzzing around her head, Granny asked, "Ya know much about the circle?"

"Not really."

"The labyrinth is a symbol of our passage through time and experience, each turn reflectin' a part of yer life. Walkin' the path is akin to takin' a journey in here." Granny placed her palm against her heart. "When yer finished, ya go back into the world with a better understandin' of yerself and what yer purpose is on this earth." She sighed. "Leastways, that's what my mama taught me and I taught Catherine."

"Did Mom sit here often?"

Granny nodded. "When Catherine was done thinkin', she'd come home and not talk fer hours. Yer papaw used to git madder'n a hornet at her sulkin'. But I knew."

"Knew what?"

"Yer mama wasn't happy livin' here no more. She wanted things yer papaw and I couldn't give her." Granny shook her head. "If I hadn't built the labyrinth, yer mama woulda never left."

Maggie doubted the circle had made any difference in her mother's decision to run away. But obviously Granny needed a reason to explain her daughter's disappearance.

Hoping for honesty, Maggie asked, "Why didn't you answer the letter Mom sent you years ago?"

Confusion showed in her grandmother's eyes. "What letter?"

Had Granny never received the missive? "When I was three, my father died, and shortly after that Mom lost her job as a receptionist for a car dealership. Mom had been frightened at the prospect of raising me on her own, and she wrote a letter asking for your permission to come home. The letter was returned unopened."

A single tear wet Granny's cheek. "I didn't get no letter."

The raw emotion in her voice and the deep sorrow in

her eyes convinced Maggie that her grandmother told the truth. "If you had, what would your answer have been?"

Grasping Maggie's hand, Granny whispered, "I'd have told my Catherine to get on back here, where she and her youngin' belonged."

Maggie wrapped an arm around Granny's frail shoulders and hugged her. "How did things get so messed up?" With her free hand, Maggie reached into her pocket and withdrew the letter in the still-sealed envelope. After her mother's death, Maggie had never been able to bring herself to read the note. "Here, Granny. It's yours now."

Gnarled fingers clutched the paper to her chest. Tears streamed from her eyes, pooling in the wrinkles on her face.

"Don't cry." Maggie shouldn't have brought up the letter. She hadn't expected her grandmother to become this upset.

An arthritic finger pointed to the writing on the outside of the envelope—Return to Sender. "That's yer papaw's scratchin'. He done sent the letter back 'n never said nothin' to me."

Granny's shoulders shook and Maggie hugged her a second time, then stood. Fighting her own tears, she said, "Don't rush. I'll wait for you at the entrance." Maggie followed the meandering path until she reached the beginning of the labyrinth, where Blue grazed on the grass. She collapsed onto the ground and lifted her face skyward. Why had her grandfather kept the letter from Granny? Had he been so embarrassed and humili-ated by his daughter's pregnancy that he refused to forgive his only child? Almost an hour passed before

Granny made an appearance. Eyes puffy and red-rimmed, she sniffed. "Where's my Catherine buried?"

"She's not." Maggie scrambled to her feet. "Mom chose to be cremated. I have her ashes at my condo."

"Time fer yer mama to come home. Ya bring her with ya when ya come visit next time." Maggie wasn't sure there would be a next time. Granny hobbled forward. "I'm headin' to the church."

"Why?" Maggie grabbed Blue's reins and trailed after.

"Got me a few things to say to Catherine's daddy."

Once they reached Granny's cabin, Maggie tethered Blue to an old hitching post in the yard, then drove Granny to the church. Maggie was dying to learn what her mother had written in the letter, but refrained from asking. If her grandmother wanted to share the note, she would when she was ready. Whatever the message, it had stirred Granny into a fit. Maggie had never seen the old woman more determined than now—lips pursed, chin jutting and hands clenched into fists.

Maggie pulled into the dirt lot adjacent to the small white church—the quintessential rural house of worship, with steeple pointing heavenward, stained-glass windows and a graveyard nestled into the hillside.

"Best you wait in the truck," Granny ordered.

"Why?"

"'Cause what I got to say ain't fit fer a young woman's ears." Granny slammed the door.

The white fence surrounding the cemetery needed painting. The grass needed trimming—the small tombstones were all but hidden by the tall blades of grass. Maggie kept an eye on her grandmother as she followed a meandering path to a marker planted under an oak tree. Granny stood with her hands on her hips for a moment, then flailed at the air, one gnarly finger jabbing at the gray block of granite.

Oh, man, was Maggie's grandfather receiving a lashing. Maggie ached for her grandmother and the pain of discovering that her daughter had sought her help, but she hadn't been there for her—all because of her husband's stubborn pride.

Men.

At that instant, any lingering reservations Maggie harbored over seeking out her grandmother vanished. It was too late for mother and daughter, but maybe not too late for grandmother and granddaughter. Regret filled Maggie that her mother had died not knowing Granny had loved her and missed her through the years. Throat aching at the sight of the grieving woman, Maggie made a promise to watch over Granny. Hopefully her mother would find peace now that Maggie had connected with her grandmother.

Maggie's gaze shot skyward, where dark clouds gathered on the horizon. Beginning tonight, the weather forecast called for thunderstorms and torrential rains. Her grandmother finished her diatribe, then returned to the truck. "God's madder'n a wet hen." She pointed to the eerie sky as she slid onto the front seat.

Once they drove from the church lot, Maggie spoke. "Think I'll have time to ride Blue over to the Kavenaghs' and return before the rain hits?" Maggie had ridden Blue to Jeb's place earlier that morning. Jeb had put up a fuss over Maggie checking his hand, but she noted the widower appreciated the attention. She'd invited her grandmother to ride along, but Granny wasn't speaking to Jeb. They'd gotten into an argument at the birthday party over, of all things, how awful the tea Granny had brewed to lower Jeb's fever tasted.

If Granny had a barn to shelter Blue during the storm, Maggie wouldn't bother returning the animal until tomorrow. But leaving the horse out in the elements wasn't an option, especially if the storm grew violent. Maggie would have to take her chances and ride Blue to the blacksmith's.

"I reckon Tom'll give ya a lift home when the storm blows over."

After arriving at the cabin, Maggie made sure her grandmother was settled before climbing on Blue and heading into the woods. She'd ridden ten minutes when the first clap of thunder rumbled. Another minute passed, then two. Maggie believed she might escape the rain when big fats drops began smacking her in the face. Thankfully the dense tree canopy kept her from getting soaked.

Maggie gripped the reins tighter, praying Blue wouldn't dump her on the forest floor then gallop off as he'd done before. About a mile from Abram's cabin, the horse picked up the path that bordered the banks of the Black River. Blue's ears perked and Maggie heard—

"Shit!"

Someone in these woods was in a foul mood. The cussing and cursing continued. Maggie wasn't sure if she was on public or private land, so she coaxed Blue deeper into the underbrush, seeking cover.

The sound of splashing accompanied the swearing. Another ten yards and Maggie stopped the gelding. A man stood with his back to her in the middle of the river, water up to his waist, searching for something. *What on earth?*

She slid off Blue and tied the reins to a tree branch, then crept closer. And closer. And… *Abram?*

Damn the man, he'd lied to her! Fury propelled Maggie forward. Instead of paying attention to where she stepped, she kept her eyes glued to the soldier. A wind gust knocked her sideways and Maggie lost her balance, falling to the ground at the edge of the river. The jarring impact knocked the air from her lungs and for a second stars danced before her eyes.

When her vision cleared, the first thing that popped into focus was a combat boot floating in the water inches from her nose. For a moment she thought Abram had crossed the river and collapsed next to her. She lifted her head, searching for a leg to go with the boot. Instead her gaze landed on a steel rod.

Confused, she scrambled to her knees and snatched the heavy boot from the water. A prosthesis? She glanced at Abram. He was still making dives below the water and hadn't spotted her. Staring at the boot, Maggie wasn't sure if she was angry or hurt that Abram hadn't confided in her.

Her mind replayed the afternoon of their picnic when he'd pushed her away the moment her foot had bumped *this* boot. Then his shocked expression at Granny's party when Maggie had admitted her ability to sense things about people. Had Abram assumed she'd been aware of his missing leg? Is that why he'd cut and run?

Did he think so little of her that he expected her to tuck tail if she discovered he'd lost a leg in the war? She stood, clasping the prosthesis—debating whether to bean Abram over the head with it or simply wait until he half drowned digging around for the missing apparatus. Neither consideration brought any satisfaction.

After an eternity, he stopped flailing in the water and struggled to the riverbank, where he threw himself in the soft mud, his breathing erratic, his lower body still in the water. Maggie waited for Abram to notice her. If he hoped ignoring her would convince her to leave, he was messing with the wrong woman. After an eternity, she cleared her throat.

He raised his head and their gazes connected.

She held up the prosthesis. "Looking for this?"

Chapter Ten

"You planning on hitting me with that?" Abram's gaze shifted to the prosthesis Maggie wielded above her head like a war club.

"I'm tempted," she muttered, lowering the prosthetic leg. "You lied to me." When he remained silent, she thunked his shoulder with the boot attached to the steel rod. "You never left the hollow, did you?"

Irritation flashed in his eyes, and he growled, "I left for a couple of days."

Pain and anger squeezed Maggie's chest, making breathing next to impossible. The churning mix of emotions inside her led her to conclude she was in deeper with the soldier than she'd estimated.

"Leave me alone, Maggie."

Ignoring the command and the deluge of rain soaking her, she asked, "What happened to your prosthesis?"

"The damn thing broke when I tried to cross the river." Abram's face darkened. "As far as I'm concerned, you can throw the useless contraption in the garbage."

Assuming the question would fuel his argumentative attitude, Maggie resisted the urge to ask how he intended to move around on one leg. "Let me help you." She inched forward but stopped short when a feral growl erupted from his mouth.

"If you really want to help, leave me alone."

With the lower half of his body still submerged beneath the cold water, Maggie worried that Abram might develop hypothermia. "The cabin's a quarter mile away. You can ride Blue. I'll walk," she offered.

Jaw clenched, he raised his face to the thunderous sky, eyes closed. "Maggie, please," he whispered, his voice hoarse. "Just leave."

The man was too prideful for his own good. If she refused to comply, he'd remain in the water until… forever. "Fine." She stormed to the tree line, where the horse waited. After tying the prosthesis to the saddle, she climbed on Blue. Before leaving, Maggie glanced over her shoulder. Abram hadn't moved from the water.

Stubborn fool.

She guided Blue deeper into the woods, then stopped when the dense trees hid her from view. There she waited. Watched. She'd give him ten minutes to haul himself out of the water, or she'd drag him up the bank herself. According to her Timex, the soldier used nine minutes and fifty-five seconds of the allotted time before he moved.

His exit from the river wasn't graceful or pretty. He slid back into the water twice before his foot found purchase on the slippery ground. From thirty yards away, the strain on his face was evident as he clawed his way up the slope, foul words flying from his mouth. Maggie's eyes burned at his struggle.

When he reached the top of the bank, he collapsed,

his chest heaving as he gulped air. After a moment, he hauled himself to a tree stump, where he sat, head in his hands. He looked forlorn and so alone sitting in the pouring rain.

C'mon, Abram, move. He'd end up with pneumonia if he didn't seek cover.

As if he heard her silent plea, he withdrew a pocket-knife from his pants. In a matter of seconds he'd cut off the left pant leg below the knee, then stood and swayed before catching his balance. Heart breaking, she watched him hop on one foot between the trees, using the trunks for balance. She and Blue followed, careful to remain hidden.

Abram had progressed twenty yards when his foot caught on something and he stumbled. Unable to regain his balance, he fell. Not even the rumble of thunder masked the *thud* when his body hit the ground. Maggie swallowed a gasp. If he didn't move soon, she'd ride Blue to his side and insist he get on the horse. Abram never gave her the chance. He crawled to his knees, hauled himself up and zigzagged through the forest. He'd almost arrived at the edge of the woods near his cabin when he stumbled again. Instead of struggling to stand, he dragged himself to the yard. Maggie flinched as she envisioned the abuse his knees were taking—torn flesh and bruised bones.

The cabin sat fifty yards away—an insurmountable distance to a man with one leg. Abram managed to stand, then hopped several feet. Rested. Hopped again. Rested. Slowly but surely, he crossed the open ground. Just when she believed he was home safe, he fell at the bottom of the porch steps.

Oh, Abram. How much more can you take?

Maggie quieted Blue when he snorted.

Get up. C'mon, you can do it.

But this time he couldn't. He crawled, one agonizing inch at a time. When he made it to the door, he used the handle to haul himself upright. The door swung open, but before Maggie breathed a sigh of relief, his foot bumped the threshold and he pitched forward, his upper body landing inside the cabin, his leg sticking out the door.

Tears poured from Maggie's eyes. *Don't give up, Abram.* A minute passed and he remained motionless. Enough was enough. He'd proved his point—he didn't need her. But if he assumed she'd walk away and leave him in such a sorry state, he didn't know her at all.

After tying Blue to a tree where the horse would be protected from the downpour, she sprinted across the clearing. She stepped over Abram's body and collapsed to her knees to examine his head and face. His eyes remained closed, but he moaned when she pressed her fingertips to the bloody cut along his jaw. He must have hit his chin on the floor.

His face and hands were scratched and Maggie yearned to pull him into her arms and heal his wounds with kisses and hugs—even the injuries that weren't visible. His lashes fluttered up and for an instant Abram allowed her a glimpse into his soul. The pain and agony took her breath away. At that instant Maggie realized her feelings for Abram had rushed past caring and hovered dangerously on the precipice of love.

"I need to clean these cuts or they'll become infected," she whispered, silently cursing the wobble in her voice. She blinked, refusing to cry. Abram needed her strength, not her tears.

AH, MAGGIE. WHY won't you leave me alone?

Abram steeled himself against the concern in her shimmering eyes. With a shaking hand, he stroked her cheek. Getting himself to the cabin had taken every ounce of strength he'd possessed. He had nothing left with which to fight her. "You'd make a hell of a soldier, Maggie O'Neil."

"Let's get you into a chair." She helped him roll over and sit up. He waved her off when she reached for his arm. Relying on sheer stubbornness, he lifted himself onto the chair Maggie had positioned behind him. Through heavy-lidded eyes, he observed her close the cabin door, then rummage through the kitchen cabinets until she located the first-aid kit.

Hell. He hadn't wanted her to find out about his missing leg—not this way.

Then what way? You would have never told her.

Damn right he'd have kept it a secret. He hadn't wanted to appear imperfect, not in Maggie's eyes. Now, besides being flawed, he looked stupid. He hated that she'd stood on the riverbank watching him thrash like an idiot in the water, then followed him as he struggled to reach to the cabin.

Maggie went into the bedroom, then reappeared in the doorway and announced, "You need a hot shower before I see to the scratches on your face." Her eyes dropped to his missing leg. "And your knees."

You can touch my face, Maggie, but you're not touching my legs.

"The cut along your jaw won't stop bleeding until I stitch it." She stood before him. "Don't fight me, Abram. This is one battle I intend to win."

"I'll clean up as soon as you leave," he promised.

She crossed her arms over her chest, drawing his attention to her wet, clinging shirt. "I'm not going until you've showered and your wounds have been tended to."

He was tempted to call her bluff, but the sparks in her eyes insisted she wasn't blowing smoke. "I can wash myself." He stood on his good leg. After a ten-second glare-down, Maggie retreated and puttered with the dishes in the kitchen sink while he hopped into the bedroom, then slammed the door.

Thank God the Monroes had installed a generator to heat the cabin's water. The hot shower went a long way toward defrosting his icy limbs. He sat on the small seat inside the stall and closed his eyes as steam billowed around his head and the pulsating water pummeled his aching muscles.

Why couldn't Maggie have kept her distance? After Granny's birthday party he'd acknowledged that he couldn't pretend forever that Maggie would never discover the truth about his disability. Years down the road when Maggie thought about Abram he'd wanted her to remember his kisses and their afternoon at the stock-car race—not his struggle to make it to his cabin on one leg.

Although he wished to remain angry at Maggie for butting in where she wasn't appreciated, a part of him gladly accepted the help she offered. When was the last time anyone had shown such sincere concern? After soaping himself twice, he rinsed, then turned off the water. A towel had been placed on the toilet lid and clean clothes underneath it. As he struggled into his pants, he decided he was too damn tired to care that she'd invaded his privacy and entered the bathroom. When he opened the door, he found Florence Nightingale waiting on the edge of the bed. She'd exchanged her own wet clothes for one of his T-shirts and a pair of sweat pants.

Face solemn, Maggie moved forward and shoved her shoulder under his armpit, then helped him to the table in the main room. As soon as he sat, she blotted the oozing blood on his jaw with a damp rag, then slapped a Band-Aid over the cut and placed a sandwich on the table before him. "Eat," she commanded.

Why did women believe food was the answer to everything that ailed a man? While he ate, she disinfected a needle and thread from the first-aid kit.

"If you prefer, I can numb the area with ice."

"Go ahead and stitch it." The sooner Maggie finished, the sooner she'd leave. He pushed the empty plate away and faced her.

"Hold still," she instructed, removing the Band-Aid.

He winced at the sting of the first stitch, but the three after never registered. She dabbed the wound with antibiotic cream, then put on a fresh Band-Aid. "Let's check the other nicks." Her fingers caressed his forehead as she went to work on the scratches.

Abram's muscles tightened at the powerful urge to gather Maggie in his arms and bury his face in her neck. But he knew that as soon as he closed his eyes, the faces of his comrades would flash through his mind—their vacant stares and blown-up bodies reminding him that he had no right to Maggie and he sure as hell had no right to any happiness or peace in his life. He'd decided when he'd left the army that he'd live alone the rest of his days. Life would be easier, less emotional. Then Maggie had happened along, making him question his plans. Question his sanity.

Disgusted with himself for allowing her to worm her way under his hide, he shoved his chair back. "I'm fine. You can leave now."

"What about your knees?"

"They're fine," he lied. His knees hurt like hell. He'd noticed the bruising and swelling on his stump in the shower. As soon as Maggie left he'd ice it down. Holding the table for balance, he stood. "I'm tired." When Maggie didn't budge, he clenched his jaw and hopped into the bedroom, then collapsed on the bed. Ears tuned, he waited. Waited. And waited. Finally. The faint creak of the cabin door opening and closing.

Maggie had left him. And for the first time in a long time, Abram wished he wasn't alone.

"THOUGHT YOU'D RUN off with my horse," Tom Kavenagh grumbled after answering Maggie's knock on the door.

"An unexpected problem cropped up." Maggie's teeth chattered. The storm had ended a few minutes after she'd left Abram's cabin, but not before soaking the clothes she'd borrowed from Abram.

The big blacksmith frowned. "What kind o' problem?" He glanced over her shoulder, his gaze landing on Blue, hitched to the post by the barn.

"This kind of problem." She held up the prosthesis.

Eyes wide, Tom waved her inside. Maggie appreciated the hospitality. She handed over the leg, then hurried across the room and stood before the fireplace. "I hope Suzanne won't mind if I drip a little on her rug. I'm numb all over."

"Suzanne's visitin' her sister. Who's missin' a leg?"

The clan was suspicious of outsiders, but she had no one else to turn to. "Abram Devane."

"The soldier?"

She nodded. "I found him hobbling through the woods on one leg." She had no intention of going into the details of this afternoon. "I'm not sure what's broken on it, but Abram was so frustrated he'd have thrown it in the trash if I hadn't confiscated it from him."

After examining the contraption, Tom said, "One of the prongs on the three-pronged socket busted off." He propped the prosthetic against the chair.

"Can you fix it?" Maggie asked.

"I might be able to solder it back on, but why would I?"

Why would he? "I don't understand."

"The soldier's a stranger. He ain't one of us."

"Does he have to be a member of the clan to receive help?"

The sarcasm behind her question didn't escape the blacksmith's notice, and he grumped, "Don't trust the man."

"Has Abram done anything to hurt you or anyone else around here?"

"Heard he's got plans to build a huntin' lodge on that property. We don't want no city folk traipsin' through our neck of the woods."

Since when had Abram decided to build a hunting lodge? And why hadn't he said anything to her? "Who told you that?"

"Betty Sue at the café. Got a phone call from a bank feller askin' questions about the town. Said he needed the information 'cause he had a client wantin' to build a huntin' lodge nearby."

"And no one checked to see if it was Abram?"

Tom shrugged. "Only an outsider would do such a dang-fool thing."

Feeling the onset of a headache, Maggie rubbed her temple. She wanted to change into dry clothes, snuggle under her grandmother's bed quilt and have a good cry. Her own comfort would have to wait awhile longer, though. "How's Suzanne's arthritis?"

"Hurtin' like always." He narrowed his eyes. "Why?"

"If I obtained a prescription-strength medicine that would ease her pain better than Granny's liniments, would you repair the prosthetic leg?"

Rubbing his whiskered jaw, Tom murmured, "You talkin' 'bout makin' a trade?"

"That's right. Suzanne needs an antiinflammatory drug called Naprosyn. As long as your wife isn't suffering from heart disease or stomach problems, she can take the medicine." Maggie would have to phone the nurse at the clinic again and ask her to over-night sample packets of the drug. "If the medication helps, I'll write Suzanne a prescription so she can continue taking it." Maggie was counting on Tom's love for his wife to sway him.

He didn't disappoint. "I'll see what I can do about the leg."

"Thanks." She moved to the door.

"Suppose you'll be wantin' Blue tomorrow."

"Not until I have Suzanne's pills. Won't be more than a day or two." She motioned to the prosthetic. Will that be enough time?"

"I reckon so." He slipped a set of keys off the hook by the door. "I'll give you a ride to Granny's." They were halfway to his truck, when he stopped. "You ain't gonna tell Granny about the pills, are you?"

"Not as long as you don't tell anyone about Abram's leg."

"I can keep a secret if you can." A corner of Tom's mouth tilted a fraction and Maggie returned his smile. She and the blacksmith had taken the first tentative steps toward friendship.

MAGGIE WAVED HER THANKS to Tom as he drove off, then faced her grandmother, who guarded the doorway, wearing a disgruntled expression. Night had fallen a half hour ago and she had expected Granny might worry over her granddaughter's whereabouts.

"I can explain everything," Maggie announced when she drew within hearing range.

As soon as she made it to the stoop, Granny looked her up and down and accused, "Ya went to see that no-good soldier, didn't ya?"

"Do I have to stay out here in the cold and have this conversation, or may I get out of these wet clothes before I end up with pneumonia?"

For a moment, Maggie wondered if her grandmother would banish her from the cabin. Then, with a grunt, Granny retreated inside and Maggie followed, shutting the door behind her. Maggie decided to get their confrontation over with before changing clothes. "Yes, I went to see Abram."

Granny reclaimed her rocker by the window. Once she was settled, Maggie continued. "The day of your surprise birthday party, Abram announced he planned to leave the hollow. I decided to check for myself, so I went the long way around to the blacksmith's." She glanced at her grandmother. "Turns out that he'd left for a couple of days but then came back."

"Ya stay away from him."

How can I avoid Abram when I'm falling in love with him? "You're not even acquainted with him, Granny."

"Don't need to be."

Reminded of her grandmother's gift, Maggie asked, "Do you 'see' something in him that I don't?"

Twisting her hands in her lap, Granny refused to make eye contact.

"You *can't* see him. That's why you don't trust him."

Exhibiting a burst of energy, Granny flew from the rocker, grabbed the fireplace poker and began prodding the burning wood. "I didn't see my own child's death. I shoulda felt it in here—" Granny pounded a fist against her chest "—that my Catherine was ailin'."

The anguish in her grandmother's voice tugged at Maggie's heart. Granny was losing the one talent that had defined her all her life. The clan counted on the old woman's sight to protect them, and like any elder in a position of responsibility, Granny fretted over her charges. Without a family of her own, the old woman needed to be needed. Maggie had no doubt in her mind, as well, that Granny didn't wish to be a burden to others.

"Isn't it natural to lose some of that ability as you age?" Maggie was at a loss at how to comfort her grandmother.

"Don't rightly know. My granny died afor she turned sixty."

"Maybe if I tell you about Abram, it will put your mind at ease."

"No matter what ya say. He can't be trusted 'cause he ain't one of us."

"Neither am I, Granny. I wasn't born or raised in the hollow."

"I knows that, but ya got the blood of the Scotch-Irish runnin' through yer veins. And ya can sense things." Granny slapped her palm against her breast again. "In here, yer one of us. Yer mama tried to ignore it, but ya can't run from who ya are."

"That's what this is all about, isn't it, Granny? My mother."

"If yer mama hadn't run off with that no-good...she woulda come to her senses 'bout belongin' here."

"You believe I'm just like my mother. That I'll split with Abram for good." Granny's silence was answer enough. "I'm thirty years old. Old enough to make my own decisions about whom I want to be with. And nothing you say or do will change my mind about Abram. He's a nice man. An honorable man." *A man who's hurting. A man I want to heal. A man I'm falling in love with.*

A man who keeps pushing you away.

Maggie was too tired to argue with her grandmother. Besides, Granny worried for nothing. Abram had made it clear that he wasn't interested in a future with Maggie.

"If you see that feller again, ya grab yer bags and go."

Maggie sucked in a surprised breath. "You're kicking me out?"

Granny's chin jutted, but Maggie detected fear in the old woman's eyes—fear that her granddaughter would take her at her word.

"Is this how you treated my mother?" Maggie regretted the remark as soon as it slipped from her mouth. "I promise, Abram wants nothing to do with me."

"Then he's lyin'. I seen the way he looks at ya."

Deep in her heart, Maggie believed that Abram had feelings for her—though what kind and how deep he'd never reveal. "He might care, but he won't do anything about it. If I seek him out, it will be in a nursing capacity, nothing more."

"What's ailin' him?"

"It's personal, Granny. I can't say."

"Don't make me no never mind. Can't trust the feller."

"The real problem is that you don't trust *me*."

"If yer mama had listened—"

"Mom would have still left."

The blood drained from her grandmother's wrinkled face.

"The best you can do is love your children, then let them go." Maggie disappeared into the bedroom, wondering if she should accept her own advice. If she let Abram go, would he find his way back to her when he figured out that she was what made him happy?

This past week, when she'd thought Abram had left the hollow, Maggie had toyed with the idea of moving in with her grandmother permanently. Granny wasn't the easiest person to rub shoulders with, but she was family—the only family Maggie had left.

Maggie never would have figured she'd tire of working at the satellite clinic in Louisville, but she'd found a sense of satisfaction in helping Jeb and again in promising to help Tom's wife, Suzanne. The idea of assisting her grandmother in caring for the clan appealed to Maggie. Her nursing skills could make a difference in this small Appalachian community.

But now that Abram intended to build a hunting

lodge on his property, she wasn't certain she cared to live in his backyard—not when he'd made it clear he didn't want her in his life.

Chapter Eleven

Maggie sat astride Blue, hidden in the trees beyond Abram's cabin. Three days had passed since she'd stitched his chin and had left with his prosthetic leg. This morning she'd driven into Finnegan's Stand and picked up the samples of Naprosyn and a sleeve for Abram's stump that Maggie's co-worker had mailed to the post office. True to his word, Tom Kavenagh had repaired the broken prong on the apparatus and had tightened the screws and bolts that had loosened over time.

While in town, Maggie had contacted the dealership for an update on her car and the manger had assured her that the Honda would be ready by Saturday. The end of September was fast approaching, and soon she'd have to return to her job in Louisville.

Now that Abram's missing leg was out in the open, they had two choices: deal with it or ignore it. Abram would choose to ignore it.

I'm choosing to deal with it.

Nudging her heels against Blue's side, she guided the horse out of the woods. As they crossed the field, the late-afternoon sun blinded her and she couldn't tell if Abram watched from any of the windows.

After securing Blue to the porch rail, she retrieved the prosthetic leg and knocked on the door. *Silence.* She knocked again. More silence, then… "Go away, Maggie."

Heart beating double time, she insisted, "I'm not leaving." When she tried the handle, the door swung open.

Abram sat at the table, sketching on a large notepad. He didn't acknowledge her presence, probably hoping that if he ignored her, she'd disappear. Swallowing her annoyance, she held out the leg. "It's fixed."

She wasn't sure what reaction she expected from Abram but it wasn't the blank stare he leveled over her shoulder. She set the prosthesis on top of the drawing pad. "I also brought along these." Two silicone liners to protect his stump. "If you prefer, I'll wait outside…"

Her comment drew a surprised glance from him. He swallowed hard. Maggie ached to soothe the wounded warrior's battered soul, but they both knew that no matter how frustrated and angry Abram was at having lost a limb, he was better off using a prosthetic device than hopping around like a one-legged chicken.

"I can't," he muttered.

Maggie blinked the stinging moisture from her eyes. Did he always have to be so tough on himself?

"My leg is too bruised," he added.

"Let me see." It wasn't an offer but a command. She held her breath, willed him to comply.

To her amazement, he scooted the chair back and spun on the seat, facing her. She knelt in front of him and gently rolled the loose pant leg end over end until the material reached mid thigh. She pressed against the flesh that had been sewn together over the end of the bone. "You're right. It's swollen and bruised." *Stubborn fool*. If only he'd accepted her offer to ride Blue, instead of crawling on his knees to the cabin.

His hand trapped hers against his thigh and she lifted her gaze to his face. His tortured expression stole the breath from her lungs. She pulled her fingers free, then continued probing, checking the knee joint. Abram had been lucky he'd lost his leg below the knee—if you could call losing any part of your body lucky.

"Do you have ice?" She wasn't sure how much feeling Abram had around the knee joint, but ice would help ease the swelling.

"In the freezer." As she walked away, he asked, "Who worked on the leg?"

"Tom Kavenagh." She peeked over her shoulder and caught him inspecting the repairs. "We made a trade." She placed the ice in a kitchen towel, wet the outside, then moved over a second chair for Abram to rest his stump on. She laid the ice over his bruised flesh, then sat at the table across from him.

"What kind of trade?" he asked.

"I offered Tom prescription-strength pain medicine for his wife's arthritis. Granny's salves aren't helping Suzanne. In exchange for the pills, he agreed to work on the prosthesis."

A corner of Abram's mouth lifted. "How does Granny feel about the trade?"

"Granny doesn't know. Tom and I took an oath of secrecy."

With an appreciative nod, Abram said, "The blacksmith did a good job."

"You sound shocked."

He motioned to the sketch pad. "Betty Sue said

Kavenagh discovered I'm toying with the idea of building a year-round hunting lodge on my property and he's ticked."

He's not the only one who's upset. "Why didn't you mention a hunting lodge to me?" Maggie winced at the hurt note that resonated in her voice.

"I wasn't positive I'd find a partner for the project."

"It's a done deal then?" She held her breath.

"Not quite. But if I decide to go ahead, a retired colonel I'm friends with has agreed to invest in the project."

Casually she asked, "Would you live at the lodge year-round?"

"I'd be here more days than not, making sure the hunting parties obeyed the rules and didn't trash the area."

Maggie had her answer. Abram propsed to make his home in these mountains. That meant Maggie couldn't—not if she didn't find a way to change Abram's mind about a future together for the two of them.

"You're aware that the clan doesn't trust outsiders." Maggie imagined her grandmother's anger at the notion of hunters roaming the land that butted up to the hollow. Then she remembered Katie's walks through the woods. Parents would have to remain on guard against stray bullets finding their way into their backyards or, worse, their children.

"Where did you get the sleeves?" His eyes riveted on the packages on the table.

"The same nursing friend who sent the anti-inflammatory drug for Suzanne." Maggie unwrapped a liner. "Let's check the fit."

Abram blocked her arm. "Don't."

"Don't what?"

"Don't try to pretend this doesn't bother you." He removed the towel from his stump, the skin bright red where the ice had rested.

"Your missing a leg bothers you more than me," Maggie argued.

"Hell, yes, it pisses me off." He flung the towel of ice toward the sink. It missed, smacking the front of the cabinets before dropping to the floor, scattering cubes everywhere.

Ignoring his childish outburst, she asked, "How did you lose your leg?" His mouth sagged. "What? Is it some big military secret?"

Eyes dark with agony, he whispered, "You should go."

A world of hurt festered inside Abram. She wasn't ignorant enough to assume he'd confess every dirty detail about what had gone on in Iraq, but he had to let go of the horror before it destroyed him. "Not until you tell me what happened." She left the table and sat on the sofa. "Will you light a fire?" Her sudden chill had little to do with the cool September temperature and a whole lot to do with the hell she expected Abram to reveal.

To her relief, he didn't argue, which confirmed what she'd sensed in Abram for a while now—the need to unburden his soul. He hopped across the room, using the furniture to steady himself. Once he had the fire going, he gazed into the flames. After a stretch of time she patted the cushion next to her. "Come join me."

When he sank onto the couch, she joked, "Your balance is incredible…when you're not angry." The remark almost made him smile, lending her hope that they would both survive the road they were about to travel.

ABRAM WAS CRAZY for even considering spilling his guts, but discovering that Maggie wasn't turned off by his amputation gave him hope that she wouldn't judge him as harshly as he judged himself.

Maggie had a way about her that made him feel safe. Made him yearn to open up to her. Maybe discussing the past would unravel the knot in his gut that had been present since he'd left the war. "The day started like any other. We reviewed the previous patrol's incidents."

"Incidents?"

"We kept track of IEDs—improvised explosive devices—that we located and were able to safely detonate. We tallied the times our battalion was shot at, and the number of bad guys' days we'd ruined." At her frown, he clarified. "Enemy kills. We also counted the mortar attacks and VBIEDs—car bombs."

"You experienced all those things every day?"

The wobble in her voice forced Abram to rethink his decision to discuss the past.

"Go on." The stubborn tilt of her chin indicated she refused to cower from the truth.

"Not every day." *But most days.* "I split my battalion into three groups and assigned each to various neighborhoods around Baghdad." Thank God he'd broken the group up, or more men would have died. The men Abram had gone on patrol with that day had suffered the most losses.

"My soldiers were tired. We'd been on patrol for

twelve hours. Bad things always happen at the end of a patrol, rarely the beginning." Still, Abram had refused to use the excuse for his lapse in judgment. If anything, he should have been more alert.

"We were cruising through an area of Sadr City that had been relatively nonviolent for the past month, when a group of kids approached our Humvees."

"I'm amazed children were allowed outside," Maggie murmured.

"Many Iraqis refused to remain prisoners in their own homes. Kids are the same everywhere in the world. They want to be outside playing with friends. Usually we brought candy for them. That day we handed out soccer balls, which were a big hit."

The faces of several little boys flashed through Abram's memory. Many of the kids had picked up English phrases and a few had bragged to Abram that when they grew up, they were going to become American soldiers. But on that particular day, Abram hadn't recognized the kids who'd flagged him down. "Two boys approached me and used hand signals to convey that someone had been hurt and required help along the road outside the neighborhood. Normally we would never leave our patrol area, but I'm a sucker for kids." Abram had seen too many children pay the price for the war in Iraq and he hadn't had the heart to ignore their pleas.

"We followed the kids. As soon as our Humvees cleared the neighborhood and entered the open road, the boys dived into a ditch. My stomach bottomed out. I sent orders up the line to halt the procession, but it was too late."

Maggie grasped his hand and squeezed, but remained quiet, and for that Abram was grateful. "We took fire from both sides of the road. Three of our Humvees exploded. My medic ran to help his comrades, but he was hit by a sniper bullet. When all was said and done, I lost twelve soldiers. None of us escaped uninjured."

"Dear God, Abram. I'm so sorry."

His eyes burned, but he had no tears left. He'd cried them all in Iraq. "I should have known better, Maggie. I should have sensed the setup." After he'd received a medical discharge from the service, he'd visited the parents, wives and families of the soldiers who'd been killed under his command. He'd apologized in person for the deaths of their sons, husbands, fathers and brothers.

Maggie laid her head on Abram's shoulder and clutched his hand to her heart. She shouldn't be offering her sympathy when he'd survived and the others hadn't. Then he heard a sniffle and winced.

"Don't waste your tears on me, Maggie." His words made her cry even harder. If things were different, if he wasn't so screwed up, he'd be tempted to risk a future with Maggie. But since Iraq, he'd hardened his heart against everyone who attempted to get close.

Unable to ignore Maggie's sobs, he leaned into her warmth and buried his nose against her neck, inhaling her sweet, pure goodness. Her persistence had weakened his resolve, making him needy, reckless and wishing to lose himself in her forever. "I want you, Maggie," he said.

"Yes," she sighed. Her green orbs shone with what? Love? No, she didn't love him. Not *him*. The light in her eyes had been a trick of his imagination—probably because the little boy inside himself yearned for some-one to care about him, someone to love him.

Not someone. *Maggie.* He craved Maggie's love. Her tender touch. Her sweet kisses. He'd cherish the memories for the rest of his life, holding them close when his soul cried out in the darkest hour before dawn.

His desire for Maggie scared the crap out of him, yet thrilled him at the same time.

One delicate finger tapped his lips, shattering his defenses. Then her mouth replaced the finger, and all doubts drowned beneath her kiss. He leaned back and she followed, straddling his hips. He moaned in pleasure at the weight of her breasts against his chest.

Tangling his hands in her silky hair, he tugged gently, bringing her mouth firmly against his, and he thrust his tongue between her lips and explored.

With eyes closed and his focus on Maggie's mouth, Abram succeeded in blocking out the visions that had tortured him daily since that fateful afternoon in Sadr City.

In Maggie's arms he forgot about the war, the soldiers, the terrorists, the IEDs. He trailed kisses along her neck, laving the warm, pulsating spot at the base of her throat. She arched, silently begging. He cupped her breasts, molding the lush mounds. He whisked the cotton, long-sleeved T-shirt over her head and tossed the material behind the couch. Her feminine pink bra ignited a spark inside him and he anticipated a full-blown hard-on...

Nothing. Mentally he cursed, then forced himself to relax. He traced the swirls of lace on her bra. Nuzzled her through the fabric. She squirmed out of the flimsy piece of fabric.

"Beautiful. So beautiful." He buried his face in her softness, groaning when she pressed his head more firmly to her. Her mouth opened and she gasped for breath.

He taunted her until her hands fiddled with the buttons on his jeans. Then, like the quiet notch of a gun hammer, his heart stopped beating. He panicked and clasped her wrists.

"It's okay if we don't do more than this," Maggie assured him. "Just let me touch you."

How could he refuse her anything? With Maggie's help he removed his shirt, pants and BVDs. He sat naked on the couch, totally exposed to her eyes—pools of desire that roamed over him. Her fingers skimmed his shoulders, across his chest, around both thighs and along his right calf before finding his flaccid member. *Damn!* Maggie's kisses had aroused him before, why not now? He winced at the question in her eyes.

Thankfully she didn't voice it. "You're beautiful, Abram. All muscle and sinew and…" She touched her mouth to his and breathed the next word. "Soldier." After another heated kiss he helped her shed her jeans and panties. Her thighs were slim and flawless and the dark triangle of hair below her belly called for his attention.

Incredible. She was hot and wet and ready. He stroked the soft curls, until her breath exploded in gusts against his face. When he coaxed her breast in his mouth Maggie went wild, bucking his hand.

With his fingers and thumb he tormented her until she climaxed, her body arching…her long hair fanning his thighs. She cried out not once but twice as Abram continued to caress her. Then she collapsed against his chest. "It's never been that intense."

At her confession Abram's throat thickened. At least he'd been able to give her pleasure no other man before him had. She reached between their bodies and murmured, "You're next."

He blocked her arm. His eyes searched the floor for his pants. He wanted his pants and he wanted them now.

"Did you suffer other injuries besides your leg?"

Leave it to Maggie to get right to the point. She'd opened herself up to him and now she expected him to reciprocate. "No injury that would prevent me from making love," he answered honestly.

"What did your doctors say?" She scooted from his lap and curled into his side.

"That nothing's wrong with me physically. It's all in my head." What his shrink said was that until Abram forgave himself and moved on, his subconscious wouldn't allow him to receive pleasure of any kind—including sex. He'd like to know how the hell to put something behind him that had been branded onto his soul. Not even a lifetime of good deeds would fade a scar that deep.

Maggie wasn't sure how to respond to Abram's confession. She wished with all her heart that she possessed the ability to heal his invisible wounds. She desired to be the woman who breathed new life into him and restored his faith in himself and humankind. He'd protected others for so long. She wished with all her heart she could shield him from the hurts of the past.

She had little experience, mostly textbook knowledge, of PTSD and doubted that love alone would cure the disorder. Hoping to comfort him but believing words would fall short, she silently stroked his chest, his neck, and prayed he'd find comfort in her touch.

Abram tensed, then brushed her hands aside and leaned forward to scoop his pants from the floor.

"It's okay. We don't have to talk. Let's just sit here," she insisted. Hoping to keep him from fleeing, she rubbed her breasts against his shoulders and pressed a trail of kisses down his spine.

"Don't."

He might as well have dumped a cold bucket of water on her head. The one-word protest snagged Maggie's breath. After all they'd shared, his rejection stunned her.

"Abram—"

"Get dressed, Maggie." He shuddered. "Please."

With purposeful movements, she collected her clothes from the floor and escaped to the bedroom, leaving Abram to dress in private. After barricading herself in the small bathroom, she ran the sink faucet full blast, then sat on the toilet lid and bawled, her face buried in a towel to silence her sobs. She wept for the horrors Abram had been exposed to in Iraq. Wept for the guilt he carried inside him to this day. Wept for the pain and suffering he'd experienced from his injury. Wept for the loss of his comrades—his friends.

When the tears dried, Maggie studied her reflection in the mirror—red, puffy eyes and blotchy skin. She didn't want Abram to see her this way. After splashing water on her face, she returned to the main room. Dressed and seated at the table, Abram studied the hunting-lodge sketch. "Any news on your car?" he asked.

What? How could he sit there and act as if they

hadn't been naked on the couch with each other a few minutes ago?

"It will be ready on Saturday."

"I guess you'll leave for Louisville then." When he lifted his gaze to hers, his brown eyes were guarded.

Did he want her to leave? Or hope she'd stay? "I'm not sure. Why?" *Don't shut me out, Abram.*

"No reason other than I wanted to wish you a safe trip."

She wasn't positive if she was more disgusted with Abram for disregarding the cause of his erectile dysfunction or at herself for not forcing him to confront his PTSD. "When I'm ready to leave, you'll be the first person I tell." She marched to the door, praying for a word, a command—anything that would keep her there longer.

Nothing.

She slammed the door hard enough to startle Blue.

Maggie fumed as she rode the horse to Kavenagh's cabin. Why wouldn't Abram allow her to help him? He loved her, darn it!

He'll never go first, Maggie. He'll never say I love you until you do.

She stopped Blue when they arrived at the spot where Abram had struggled in the water. Her heart swelled with love for the stubborn man. The kind of love that endured hardship. Years in the health-care profession had taught her that wanting, wishing and praying for someone to get well wasn't always enough to guarantee it. Her mother's death had taught her not to take life for granted, because no one knew what tomorrow might bring. She recalled the letter her mother had written that had never been read by

Maggie's grandparents. All those wasted years. The hurt. Her grandmother's loneliness.

Giving up on Abram was out of the question. And she refused to allow her grandmother to dictate who she should or should not love, or where Maggie should or should not live. Whether Abram or Granny approved or not, neither had any say in her future.

Maggie alone would determine her destiny.

Chapter Twelve

Friday after school, Katie appeared on Granny's door-step with a note from her mother requesting Maggie drop by for a visit that afternoon. When Maggie asked if Granny intended to tag along, the old woman declined, muttering that she had to make a new batch of salve for the blacksmith's wife. No one had informed Granny that it wasn't her salve but the prescription medication Maggie had obtained that had eased Suzanne's pain. Katie insisted on helping Granny, so Maggie borrowed the truck and headed to the Moorelands' cabin.

When she pulled into the driveway, she spotted Sullivan on the front porch. "Hello, Maggie." His gaze scanned the yard. "Where're Katie and Granny?"

"Katie's helping Granny make a salve."

"Good. Now we won't have to worry that they'll interrupt our meeting."

As Sullivan ushered her inside, Maggie couldn't recall any mentioning of a meeting in the note. She wondered what purpose her presence would serve.

"I'm positive you've met everyone." Sullivan motioned to each person. "Tom Kavenagh, clan blacksmith. Jeb Riley, clan nuisance." The old man snickered, not in the least insulted over the remark. "And Patrick Kirkpatrick. Patrick's the manager up at the sawmill."

Their solemn stares tied Maggie's stomach in knots.

"Have a seat. I'll fetch us some drinks while the others tell you why we asked you here." Jo retreated to the kitchen, and Maggie sat on the end of the sofa. The men remained standing.

Jeb spoke first. "We're thinkin' the hollow needs a medical clinic."

Suspicious of the sudden change in attitude toward medical care, Maggie balked. "I was under the impression the clan didn't trust modern medicine."

"Those pills you offered Suzanne are a miracle." Kavenagh cleared his throat. "She's smilin' more and gettin' out of bed on her own in the mornin'."

"I ain't too proud to admit I mighta died if ya hadn't fed that medicine into my arm." Jeb waved his hand, showing off the scar from his stitches. "Granny—she knows a powerful lot 'bout heather and herbs but nothin' 'bout the kind of medicine folks need fer serious injuries."

"When my men get hurt on the job, they lose pay if they have to take time off to drive sixty miles for an X-ray or a blood test," Patrick added. "A clinic in the hollow would benefit everyone."

Maggie swung her gaze to Sullivan. "I won't argue this area needs a health-care facility, but how will you fund it?"

"We've been researching that," Jo announced, entering the room with glasses of lemonade. As she handed out the refreshments, she said, "I phoned our state senator and chatted with a member of his staff. She referred me to the Kentucky State Office of Rural Health and they're working on a list of organizations to contact for financial aid."

Jo drank from her glass before continuing. "A problem we're facing is that most clan members, those who don't work at the mill, are uninsured. The government programs that offer Medicaid and Medicare services require the area to prove that their health care programs fit the federal profile of what's considered best for rural America."

"And that is…?" Maggie prompted.

"Not Granny's homemade remedies and holistic medicines," Sullivan answered for his wife.

"Then you'll need private donations to build a clinic." Maggie had no idea where that kind of money would materialize from an area of the country where many families faced a day-to-day struggle to put food on the table.

"Sawmill's health insurance isn't good," Patrick complained. "The deductibles are high and most families don't seek medical treatment because they can't afford the co-pay, never mind the prescription-drug costs."

"We might receive a few grants, but we can't rely on them year after year." Jo shared a glance with her husband that said they'd discussed this topic often. "One of the biggest hurdles to pass is of the clan's making—we're too independent. Several of the government programs Sullivan and I investigated require the clinic and its staff to follow a prescribed protocol when treating patients. If they don't, the funding disappears. In order to ensure the rules and guidelines are met, these programs send their own doctors and nurses. The clan won't stand for that."

"And it's doubtful that the clan's small numbers would support a full-time doctor or a nurse's salary," Sullivan added.

The picture they painted appeared bleak at best, and Maggie sensed their growing frustration with their community's situation. "How do you propose recruiting a staff to work for almost nothing?"

Silence followed the question. Sullivan pretended interest in his shoes. Kavenagh drank his entire glass of lemonade in three swallows. Patrick rocked on the balls of his feet, his gaze riveted to the basket of yarn near the sofa. Jeb rubbed the stain on his shirt. Only Jo had the guts to stare Maggie in the eye and admit, "We'd hoped you'd run the clinic."

"You want me to move to Heather's Hollow?"

"We trust you. You're part of the clan." Jo sat next to Maggie on the couch. "Folks will feel more comfortable seeking your help than a stranger's."

That these people accepted her as one of them warmed Maggie's heart. But how would her grandmother react if the clan chose Maggie over her when they sought treatment?

Jo grasped Maggie's arm. "As you know, Sullivan and I are coauthoring a book about the clan and Appalachia, and we recently heard from our agent that the book has been sold to a publisher."

"Congratulations," Maggie offered. The others added their sentiments, then Jo continued. "We'll split the royalties from the book between the school and the clinic. We'll do what we can to pay you something for your services, Maggie."

The idea of assisting her mother's people appealed to Maggie, and for a moment she allowed herself to be swept up in the excitement. "Have you discussed a location for the facility?"

"Renting a place in Finnegan's Stand is out of the question. We'd have to build here in the hollow," Sullivan answered.

"The mill will contribute the wood and several of the men will donate their time to build it," Patrick promised.

"Where would the clinic be located?" Maggie had no idea of the size of the hollow. Her mother had mentioned years ago that the land was boxed in on all sides by federal or private acreage.

"Best spot's where that soldier feller's stayin'," Jeb stated.

"But Abram Devane's cabin is on private property." Maggie knew that for a fact.

"The land really belongs to Granny," Jo said. "The deed to the property was lost generations ago in a fire."

Maggie recalled her grandmother's mention of a fire when Maggie had commented on the cabin's stone fireplace.

"Your relatives lost a court battle," Jo explained. "The land was handed over to the county and sold as private property, exchanging owners over the years. No one had used the cabin for almost two years when Abram suddenly showed up. We weren't aware that he'd been gifted the property."

No wonder her grandmother was adamant Maggie keep her distance from Abram. Not only did the old woman that worry her granddaughter would run off with him and leave the clan as Maggie's mother had, but also Granny must hate the idea of Maggie associating with the person who possessed what had rightfully belonged to her ancestors. Granny must consider Maggie's association with Abram a betrayal.

"There's talk he plans to build a hunting lodge on the property. The last thing we want is strangers totin' rifles around our woods, shootin' at everythin' in sight," Kavenagh grumbled.

Maggie was torn. She sympathized with the clan's position, yet she understood Abram's desire to hold on to the one place where he felt safe after serving in Iraq. "If Abram is the legal owner, how do you propose to build a clinic on his land?"

"That's where we could use your help." Sullivan eyed his wife.

Maggie swallowed hard.

"Convince the soldier to gift the land back to the clan."

Did Jo and the others suspect there was more between Maggie and Abram than simple friendship? "Even if I got him to donate a section of his property, what about Granny? She won't consent to a clinic."

"The situation is tricky." Sullivan edged forward. "Granny has been one of the clan's esteemed elders for more than thirty-five years and her position is greatly respected. But…Granny might agree to the clinic if she recovered a portion of her land. If not, then there won't be a clinic."

A few acres of land would never pacify Granny. "I don't have much pull with my grandmother."

"Yer kin. She'll listen to ya," Jeb argued.

Maggie might be related to Granny, but that didn't mean her relationship with the old woman was on solid ground. Instinctively she knew Granny didn't trust her. Until she earned Granny's confidence, Maggie had little influence over the woman.

You could do a lot of good here, Maggie. Think of how proud Mom would be if you returned to her birthplace and took care of her people—your people.

The others waited expectantly for an answer. Even if Granny and Maggie discovered a way to coexist without driving each other nuts, Maggie wasn't certain she cared to live in Abram's backyard should things not work out between them. *What a mess.*

"I'll speak with my supervisor and the doctors I deal with in Louisville. They might be able to assist with private donations and gifts of medical equipment. But I can't promise that I'll run the clinic."

"One step at a time," Sullivan declared.

The others' faces weren't as optimistic.

ABRAM HEARD A HORSE whiney and rushed to the window. He eyed the woods beyond the cabin. When his gaze landed on Maggie riding Blue, his heart paused mid thump, then resumed its irregular beat. After he'd shut her out a few days ago, he'd been positive she'd given up on him. He'd regretted hurting her, but he'd had no other choice. The sooner she left the hollow, the sooner he'd stop hoping for the impossible—a future with her.

He'd argued with himself for hours that no woman should be saddled with a man with PTSD and all the other hang-ups Abram struggled with. Even though his gut insisted that Maggie wasn't put off by his missing limb, he believed she deserved emotional and physical intimacy. Abram feared he'd never be able to give Maggie either.

Iraq had gutted him and left him a shell of a man. Then he'd met Maggie and discovered that the war hadn't stolen everything—he still had hope. *Hope.* What a shitty souvenir. The nasty little sentiment had the power to destroy a man by showing him a glimpse of happily-ever-after. Sadly he acknowledged that wanting something badly enough—Maggie—didn't guarantee he'd receive it.

The sight of her in his doorway wearing a white sweatshirt with a Red Cross logo and a pair of tight jeans produced a yearning in him, difficult to subdue. Today her hair was up in a ponytail, the style accentuating her high cheekbones. She braved a smile, but her pretty green eyes refused to meet his. He had no one to blame but himself for the awkwardness between them.

"How's the leg working?" she asked.

Was that the sole reason for her visit—to check on his prosthesis? Swallowing his disappointment, he stepped aside so she could enter the cabin. "Works fine." When she slipped past him, he inhaled, catching the scent of sunshine, outdoors and pure, sweet Maggie. He tucked the smell into the corner of his heart and shut the door. "Thirsty?"

"No, thanks." She hovered near the kitchen table, her eyes soaking up everything but him. She appeared soft and vulnerable, and he wanted her. More than he'd wanted anything in his life. Ever. No, he wasn't worthy of her, but damn it, he was just a man—a man who wished for a do-over. A chance to change the way things had ended between them. A chance to regain his pride. A chance to show her that he was a man who could bring her much pleasure.

Inch by inch, he moved forward until their chests bumped. Cradling her face in his hands, he struggled to convey how much he desired her. Needed her. Fear that he'd never be able to let her go if he confessed his feelings held the words prisoner inside him. Only a strangled syllable escaped his mouth. He waited for a sign that she understood what he was asking.

Her lashes fluttered and her breath sighed across his mouth. The kiss was tentative, full of promise.

Apology.

Longing.

Emotion swelled in his chest. With desperation he was certain Maggie sensed, he devoured her mouth. God, he loved this woman. With heart and damaged soul, he loved Maggie O'Neil.

Loved her because she refused to be intimidated by him. Because she made him feel like a man. Made him believe his disability didn't matter. Made him believe that his sacrifices and those of his men in Iraq hadn't been for nothing.

When her arms entwined his neck and she snuggled her breasts against his chest and her pelvis against his crotch, he rejoiced in his body's escalating arousal. Admitting he loved Maggie had freed him to respond to her touch. He'd pay a hefty price later for the admission, but at the moment, with Maggie's mouth under his, he didn't care.

Slow and steady he guided her into the bedroom and stopped next to the bed. "Let me make love to you, Maggie." *Please say yes.*

In answer her fingers danced across the buttons on his shirt. Within seconds she and Abram were naked from the waist up. While his mouth paid special attention to her breasts, he removed her ponytail holder, then shoved his hands into her silky hair. Naked, chest to chest, he closed his eyes and rejoiced in the blending of their heartbeats. Then Maggie's hands reached for the snap on his jeans and he tensed.

The air in the room stilled as her fingers hovered over the material. *Trust Maggie. She'll make everything okay.* Inhaling a deep breath, he placed his hands over hers and together they lowered his zipper. He sat down on the edge of the mattress and she tugged off the pants.

She skimmed out of her jeans, leaving on her white cotton panties.

"Can we remove the prosthesis?"

"It won't bother you?"

Shaking her head, she knelt before him. "I want to get as close to you as possible, Abram. I want to lie on you, around you and in you without worrying about getting scraped or cut by metal and plastic."

"I want that, too." After another scorching kiss, he removed the prosthesis, then reclined on the bed. Maggie joined him, stretching out along his side. He opened his arms and she tumbled on top of him. "We should get rid of our underwear." He grinned.

"Definitely." She playfully nipped his chest and he bucked at the erotic sensation. Once the last of their clothing was shed, Abram stopped thinking about everything save Maggie, her sexy body and how much he desired her.

Time passed in a haze of touches, kisses, sighs and eventually loud moans. Hands and mouths bumped, collided and worked in unison to ignite fires that soon became blazes. Too caught up in the moment, Abram hadn't realized how stiff his erection had become until Maggie's hands and mouth brought it to his full attention. "I'm not going to last much longer," he groaned.

"Then we better move on to the final act."

He tweaked her buttocks. "There's a box of condoms in the bathroom cabinet."

"Were you planning on some wild partying in the mountains, soldier?"

"I bought them after the stock-car race. I didn't expect to ever use them, but I'd dreamed of making love to you that night," he confessed.

Her smile lit up her face as she bounced off the bed and retrieved the birth control. In a matter of seconds she had him sheathed. He rolled her beneath him, intent on taking control. With a few adjustments he entered her in a single thrust. Maggie's back arched off the bed and he accepted that as an invitation to feast on her breasts. His lovemaking might have lacked finesse, but Maggie's wild gyrations conveyed that he pleased her. With her legs wrapped around his waist, he thrust faster, harder.

"I love you," she panted into his mouth.

Three simple words set him free and together they soared to a place in the universe where only warmth, goodness and rightness existed.

In the aftermath, Abram rested on his side and snuggled Maggie. Her declaration of love had been bittersweet. For a moment in time she'd done what no other person had been able to do—break him out of the prison he'd voluntarily thrown himself into when he'd left Iraq. But admitting that he returned Maggie's feelings would lead to making promises he wasn't positive he could keep. "I'd figured you'd returned to Louisville."

"I wouldn't leave without saying goodbye first."

No, she wouldn't. It just went to show how much better a person Maggie was than him. "When do you expect to head home?"

She stiffened and he cursed his bluntness. Part of him wished for her to stay in his arms forever. The other part wanted her gone yesterday.

Maggie propped herself up on an elbow and stared him square in the eye. "I'm contemplating moving to Heather's Hollow permanently."

Panic crawled up his throat, threatening to choke him. "Why?" He winced at the flicker of hurt in her eyes before she blinked it away.

"The clan's going to build a health clinic in the hollow and they'd like me to run it."

Now it was Abram's turn to tense. Silence enveloped the room as he struggled to formulate a response. The hollow was too small for both him and Maggie. It was bad enough to have the memory of their lovemaking haunt him the rest of his life—but the idea of bumping into her each time he was in the area checking on the lodge… *No!*

"We have one problem," Maggie added.

Only one? He envisioned a hundred conflicts with Maggie managing a health clinic and him a hunting lodge.

"They'd like to build the clinic on land owned by someone outside the clan." She quirked an eyebrow and his stomach sank as the truth registered.

"My land."

"It's not really your property, Abram."

Confused, he frowned. "I'm in possession of the deed."

"Your acreage once belonged to my grandfather's

family. Several generations back, a house fire destroyed the deed. When squatters settled the area, my ancestors went to court, but without the legal document, the judge declared the land public property. Since then it's been sold several times over."

The suspicious glances from clan members and Granny's less-than-hospitable attitude toward Abram made sense now. "No wonder your grandmother can't stand the sight of me."

"Would you consider giving back a portion of the property to Granny?"

Damned if he did and damned if he didn't. Abram shifted away from Maggie and sat up. "What happens if I don't hand over the land to Granny?"

Joining him on the side of the bed, Maggie nuzzled her cheek against his shoulder. "They'll find another place to build the clinic. Worse-case scenario, they'd build on Granny's property."

"Sounds like you're definitely staying."

"That depends."

Sweat broke out across his brow. "On…"

"I love you, Abram."

Her reiteration of her feelings gripped Abram's insides and twisted painfully. He wanted to confess those same words to her, but he choked. In self-defense, he argued, *You'll never know if her feelings for you are real or anchored in pity. She's a nurse. It's in her blood to care about people.* He clung to the notion, desperate to believe anything that would prevent him from exposing his soul to her. Handing his heart to Maggie for safekeeping meant he'd never survive if she left him. He could live without a leg but not without a heart.

"I know you care for me, Abram." She caressed his

cheek and forced him to meet her gaze. "Please give us a chance."

Throat aching, he buried his face in her neck and sucked in gulps of air, praying he wouldn't lose it. He yearned to tell her how beautiful she was. How he admired her and respected her. How he wished with all his heart he had the courage to trust in her love. But his happiness wasn't meant to be. And Maggie sure as hell warranted better than him—a man unable to love without fear. Fear that he'd never heal enough to be the kind of man Maggie needed.

He wasn't aware of how long he clung to her, his labored breathing filling the room. Finally he shifted away and reached for his prosthesis.

"So this is it? The end?" she whispered.

Abram shuddered at the stark note in her voice. He'd hurt her terribly, but better now than later when she discovered she'd wasted herself on a man who was going nowhere fast. He swallowed a moan at the tears in her eyes. *Goddamn.* What had he done to her?

When he remained silent, she collected her clothes and retreated to the bathroom, shutting—make that slamming—the door in his face. He deserved nothing less.

While she dressed, he did the same, then escaped to the kitchen. By the time she came out of the bedroom, he was standing by the window his back to her. The coward that he was, he didn't wish to see her face when she walked out. *Run, Maggie. Run before you become a prisoner in my own personal hell.*

Or stay. Force me to take a chance on you. On us.

He waited for a goodbye.

The cabin door opened, then closed with a quiet *click*.

"Ya been mopin' round here fer hours. Somethin' ailin' ya?' Granny asked.

Abram was ailing Maggie. "I'm fine," she insisted.

Less than twenty-four hours ago, she'd been wrapped in a soldier's arms, feeling loved and cherished. Now a cold emptiness seeped into every pore of her body. Abram touched her heart in a way no other man ever had. Yes, she admitted that she'd been drawn to him because she'd sensed a wounded soul inside his strong body. And yes, when she'd discovered he'd lost a leg in combat, she'd experienced a swell of compassion for the big lug and his struggle to accept his physical disability.

Compassion and a need to help others were at the core of her being. Maggie suspected that Abram believed her love for him was tangled with her need to nurture and heal. Convincing him otherwise was a battle she wasn't certain how to fight.

"Is it that soldier again?" Granny pestered. She touched a finger to her temple. "I'm sensin' somethin' powerful happened. He done somethin' I should know about?"

Good Lord. Maggie had no desire to confess that she and Abram had made love yesterday. "He's fine." Refusing to engage in a conversation about her love life, she decided now was as good a time as any to mention the clinic. "What would you say if I told you some of the clan members believe a health clinic in the hollow is a good idea?"

"Darnedest fool thing I ever heard of," Granny sputtered.

Maggie had anticipated the reaction. "The clan has a

right to modern medicine as well as the holistic remedies you provide for illnesses and other ailments."

"Ain't nothin' I can't handle." After a lengthy silence Granny dropped her gaze to the floor.

They both knew she hadn't been able to *handle* the cut on Jeb's hand. "The clinic won't replace you. The clan will continue to seek your care and advice." At least, Maggie hoped they would. In truth, she antici- pated the younger generation choosing a nurse-practi- tioner over Granny.

Maggie attempted to view the clinic from the per- spective of her grandmother—a woman whose entire life had centered on healing her neighbors. Granny had nothing to do with her time and no family, save Maggie, to fuss over. Caring for the clan made her feel useful. Growing old was difficult enough. Then to learn you were being replaced…

"They'll need your help at the clinic, Granny. I've never seen a better stitch than yours. They'll teach you to draw blood and administer shots."

"What do ya mean—*they?* Ain't ya runnin' the clinic?"

Shifting under her grandmother's narrowed-eye glare, Maggie answered, "No." Not after her falling-out with Abram.

"Ya tellin' me ya ain't stayin'?"

And live right under Abram's nose? The idea sent a stab of pain through Maggie's heart. "I prefer a real toilet over an outhouse," she joked.

Her grandmother didn't laugh. "Yer fixin' to run like yer mama."

"This has nothing to do with Mom, Granny."

"Then it got to do with me, don't it?"

Did Maggie dare confess the truth? If she didn't, her grandmother would believe that *she* was the reason Maggie intended to leave. Maggie refused to allow the old woman to live with the guilt of thinking she'd chased off both her daughter and her granddaughter.

"The truth is, Granny, I'm leaving because of Abram."

"I told ya to stay away from that soldier."

"I'm a grown woman. I'll do what I please. But that's beside the point. Abram's converting his cabin into a year-round hunting lodge." That Abram hadn't offered to return a portion of the property to the clan for the clinic told Maggie that she didn't mean as much to him as he did to her.

Granny propped her knobby knuckles on her hips. "We don't need no flatlanders prowlin' these woods, shootin' at squirrels."

Maggie agreed, but… "The land belongs to Abram and it's his to do with as he pleases."

"What's his buildin' a huntin' lodge got to do with ya leavin'?"

Maggie's eyes burned. "I fell in love with him, but Abram doesn't love me."

Chapter Thirteen

Maggie entered her nursing supervisor's office, hoping for good news. "Any leads on funding the clinic?" She'd enlisted Kathy's help as soon as she'd returned to Louisville. The woman had connections throughout the city's medical community. At sixty years of age, Kathy had put in more nursing hours than anyone at Baptist Hospital East, including the doctors.

Kathy ran the nursing staff like a military sergeant, and only the toughest and most stalwart of nurses survived under her command. Because of her dedication to the profession, she had accumulated a long list of supporters and sponsors. She rubbed shoulders with the bigwigs in the fund-raising departments at several community hospitals and was tight with drug-company representatives.

"As a matter of fact, I've received some substantial gifts of money from corporate and private sectors." Before Maggie became too excited, Kathy added, "But there's a catch."

"Which is…?"

"We've acquired enough funds to get the clinic off the ground and maintain it for maybe a year." Kathy tossed her pencil onto the desk calendar. "But there's no money to pay a health-care professional's salary."

"That's a pretty big catch," Maggie murmured. The odds of finding an intern or recent nursing graduate willing to move to an off-the-beaten-path location and run a health clinic for free weren't in their favor.

"The cost of equipment alone is double a doctor's yearly salary," Kathy insisted. "On a positive note, one of my drug reps is willing to supply the clinic with meds for diabetes, high blood pressure, and cholesterol. And I've got another rep checking into donating general antibiotics and birth control."

"What if recently graduated nurses had to do a three-month rotation at the clinic?" Maggie was certain the clan members would not appreciate strangers treating them, but what other choice did they have?

"Nope, that won't work. Young kids today are spoiled. They'd view three months without a mall, a movie theater and fast-food restaurants as a prison sentence. Regardless, the clinic requires someone who's able to write prescriptions. There's only one solution, and truthfully I hate it."

"What's that?"

"*You* have to run the clinic."

Maggie's chest tightened. "Me?"

"You're the best nurse-practitioner I have on staff. There's no one I'd trust more to manage a satellite clinic. The clan will feel comfortable asking for help from one of their own."

When Maggie didn't immediately respond, Kathy said, "Besides, you haven't been the same since you returned from Heather's Hollow."

The assessment concerned Maggie. To her knowledge she hadn't shirked her duties or made any mistakes. "What do you mean?"

"You're quiet. Too quiet. Something happened up in those mountains. Whatever it was, you're still bothered by it."

Not something—*someone*. Abram had happened to Maggie.

"Louisville is no longer for you." One gray eyebrow lifted, daring Maggie to argue.

"I miss Granny." Not an hour in the day went by when Maggie didn't wonder how her grandmother fared. Or if the old woman missed her granddaughter. Or how Suzanne's arthritis was. Or if little Katie was sneaking off into the woods alone. But mostly she wondered about Abram.

Dear God, she loved the man. Why did she have to go and lose her heart to him? Soldiers were nothing but trouble.

Abram's worth the trouble.

Kathy interrupted Maggie's reverie. "Feel free to tell me to shut up, but I'm sensing you're not happy here in Louisville."

"A lot has happened in the past year," Maggie acknowledged.

"Agreed. You've lost your mother. Reconnected with your grandmother and your mother's people. But there's more to your moping than that."

Time to fess up. Maggie blew out a deep breath and made eye contact with her supervisor. "I met a man while I was staying with my grandmother."

"Is he a member of the clan?"

"No. He lives in a cabin near the hollow. He's recuperating from a war injury he sustained in Iraq."

"What kind of wound?"

"He lost his left leg below the knee."

Kathy fell silent, not judging or jumping to conclusions. As she did every day on the job, she waited for all the facts before determining a plan of action—in Maggie's case, offering advice.

"Things didn't work out between us, but it has nothing to do with his missing leg."

"Go on."

"Abram intends to stay in the area and convert his cabin into a hunting lodge."

"You mean to tell me those mountains are too small for both of you?"

Frowning, Maggie protested, "One of us had to leave."

Kathy removed her glasses and set them aside. "Are you positive it's over between you two?"

No. At least not for Maggie. "I told Abram that I was in love with him."

"And…?"

"He didn't say anything." His silence had wounded Maggie deeply. Her reaction to his rejection had convinced her more than ever that her feelings for him were real and honest. A forever kind of love.

"How's he handling his amputation?" Kathy probed.

"Not well. He told me what had happened to his unit in Iraq, and I got the impression that he believes he should be miserable, since he blames himself for the deaths of the men under his command."

"PTSD?"

"Yes." With an exasperated sigh, Maggie admitted, "I don't have any experience with the disorder to recognize if Abram's case is typical or atypical."

"My neighbor's son-in-law lost both feet in a road-side bomb."

Shuddering, Maggie asked, "How did he handle his rehabilitation?"

"He demanded his wife of five years divorce him as soon as he was stateside. He didn't want to be a burden."

"Did they divorce?"

"No. Cindy got in his face and told him he hadn't even seen combat until he witnessed her on a rampage." Kathy grinned. "It's been a tough road for the couple, but they're still together."

"I'm not certain that I have that kind of power over Abram."

"You two never…?"

Resisting the urge to pat her burning face, Maggie confessed, "We made love. The first time…he couldn't. But the second time we tried, everything worked fine."

"Nothing unusual." At Maggie's frown, Kathy explained. "PTSD does quite a number on the mind. Has he hooked up with a therapist?"

Imagining Abram talking with a shrink brought a smile to Maggie's face. "He's the kind of man who'd rather prove he can do it on his own than accept help." She told herself to keep her mouth shut, but a part of her demanded she voice her fear. "I'm not sure he wishes to get better."

"Survivor guilt. He needs a reason to go on. Does he have one?" The eyebrow lifted again. When Maggie didn't answer, Kathy asked, "If he had *you,* would he seek help for his PTSD?"

"Abram doesn't want me," Maggie protested.

"You're certain?"

What were the chances that Abram might have rejected Maggie simply because he'd desired her? What if the reason he'd pushed her away was that he wouldn't allow himself to accept her love? What would he do when he discovered she refused to quit on him...on them?

There was one way to find out. She sucked in a trembling breath. "I believe you've found a nurse to manage the hospital's newest satellite clinic."

ABRAM FELT AS IF HE hovered on the edge of a precipice instead of the clearing that opened to Granny's labyrinth. He'd been staying in the shadows, waiting for Maggie's grandmother to finish whatever it was she was doing. The old woman hadn't budged from her seat on the stone bench in the center of the circle, surrounded by amethyst heather fields. Every few minutes she'd glance at the sky as if communicating with a spirit beyond the clouds.

Her slight build and hunched frame were deceiving to the casual observer. Granny was a force to be reckoned with, and one that Abram had come to the conclusion he had to confront. He edged closer, intentionally making noise to warn her of his presence. When Granny's gaze remained rooted to the ground, he assumed old age had made her hard of hearing. After all the bombs that had detonated near him in Iraq, Abram had already suffered some loss of hearing.

When he was within fifteen feet of her, he stopped and cleared his throat.

"'Bout time ya showed up," she muttered.

Her directness unnerved Abram. Had Granny seen into his mind and heart this past week? Was she aware of his inner turmoil? "Mind if I sit?"

She moved her skirt aside and he made do with the small space she offered. Abram didn't know where to begin, so he settled on asking a question. "Did you build this labyrinth?"

"Me and Maggie's mama."

"What do all the different paths mean?"

Granny tilted her head and leveled a squinty-eyed stare at him.

"Ever walked a labyrinth?"

"No, ma'am."

"Best come on then." Abram followed her, and after the first turn, she explained. "It's like takin' a walk through yer life. Each ring is a symbol fer somethin' ya done. While yer walkin', yer thinkin'."

"About what?"

"'Bout life. Folks. Regrets. Dreams. Ya ought to do a bit of repentin', too."

In order to confess all his regrets, Abram would need to walk the circle the rest of his life.

"We're goin' the wrong way, but I figure that's fittin' since ya done gone 'bout everythin' ass backward with my granddaughter."

Abram swallowed a protest, then asked, "What should I contemplate?"

"Ya start with yer birth, then work through the years. By the time ya git to the center, ya figured out what's gotta be fixed. Then ya make the journey back out into the world again a better person."

When they reached the entrance of the labyrinth, Granny stopped. "Now, git yer head on straight and start thinkin'." She left Abram and returned the way they'd ventured. He gave her a head start, then forced his mind to shift to the days of his youth. With each step he noted nothing spectacular about his childhood. He'd had friends, food, clothes and shelter. Maybe his parents hadn't doted on him, but they'd cared as much as their advanced age and busy lives had allowed.

After his childhood had come adolescence, high school, college. Each face or incident that flashed through his mind appeared with an emotion—anger, regret, fury, hurt, happiness. When he made it to the bench, he was emotionally gutted, yet filled with a sense of peace. He claimed his seat next to Granny.

"Ya cheated," she accused him.

How the hell did a person cheat walking a circle that had no outlet? "What are you talking about?"

"Ya didn't think 'bout everythin'."

Had she suspected that he'd purposefully omitted thoughts of Maggie? He hadn't contemplated her because he hadn't wanted to torture himself with what-ifs. "I don't want to talk about your granddaughter."

"Wasn't referrin' to Maggie."

Good God the old woman was a trial. "What or who are you referring to then?"

"Yer soldierin'."

"No offense, Granny, but I won't discuss my time in Iraq and I sure as hell try not to think about."

"I knows that. Seems to me ya gotta face the past before ya can move on to the future."

"I am living in the future. That's why I'm here. I have a proposition for—"

"We'll git to that reason in a minute. First things first. When ya gonna stop blamin' yerself for somethin' that was outta yer hands and in the Lord's?" Granny frowned.

"Maggie told you about what happened in Iraq?" It was bad enough Maggie knew. He didn't want—

"No, my granddaughter ain't said nothin' 'bout nothin' where yer concerned. But I believe somethin' powerful bad happened to ya."

What purpose did it serve to pretend the past hadn't happened? "Sixteen good men lost their lives because of me."

Granny, thank God, stayed silent.

Abram recounted the story of the ambush, and after a stretch of silence, Granny asked, "If ya hadn't listened to the youngin's and left the neighborhood, what do ya think would have happened?"

Abram hadn't considered that. "Can you see it in your mind, Granny?"

She shook her head. "I feels it mostly."

"Feel what?"

"Ya sure ya care to hear?"

"Why wouldn't I?"

"'Cause then ya ain't got no excuse fer bein' an ass."

Christ, the old biddy shot from the hip. "Heaven forbid I be something other than an ass. Tell me."

"They'd a still attacked ya. Ya might not have lost yer men, but a lot more kids and womenfolk woulda died. I reckon yer actions saved a whole lot of people."

Abram wanted to believe his men hadn't died in vain, that they'd sacrificed themselves for the greater good.

"Now ya know ya couldn't have done nothin' different. Time ya quit feelin' sorry fer yerself."

"It's not that easy, Granny."

"Nothin' worth havin' in life is easy, young man."

He considered how Maggie had bared her soul, confessing her love for him. He'd held those precious words close to his heart, believing he wasn't worthy of them. "How's Maggie?" he inquired, attempting to work his way up to asking Granny's permission to see Maggie. He hoped for a chance to redeem himself in her eyes before she went back to Louisville.

"Can't say. She done left the hollow."

Stunned, Abram croaked. "When?" Maggie had promised she wouldn't leave without saying goodbye.

"Last week. Tom drove her up to get her car. Maggie said there weren't room fer the both of ya here."

"As much as I love these mountains, they're more Maggie's than mine. But that's beside the point. I came here today to tell you that you can have your land back. Maggie explained about your ancestors owning the property before the Civil War and then losing the deed to it in a fire."

He thrust his hand into his pants pocket and retrieved the title to the property the previous owners had gifted him. He'd already contacted the Monroes and discussed the situation. They'd given their consent to return the land to the clan. He placed the deed in Granny's lap. "It's yours now, Granny. Maggie mentioned the cabin was a good spot to build a clinic."

"I heard talk 'bout buildin' one of those fancy medical clinics with all them newfangled machines. It's true I'm gittin' long in the tooth, but I don't like it one bit that folks is losin' the old ways."

"Maggie's a good nurse. She'll make sure the old ways are respected."

"What if she don't come back?" For the first time during their conversation, Granny's voice cracked with emotion. Underneath the elderly woman's gruff exterior was a lonely grandmother who missed her granddaughter.

One way or another Abram would bring Maggie

home. Whether things worked out between them or not, Maggie belonged in Heather's Hollow. "She might visit again if you put plumbing in your cabin," he teased.

A glint of hope lightened her eyes. "Ya reckon ya can put in a crapper fer me?"

After he and his soldiers had been forced to dig temporary toilets or burn barrels in Iraq, installing a commode ought to be easy. "I'd be proud to be your crapper man, Granny."

"Soons ya get the gadget hooked up I got one more job fer ya."

"What's that?"

"Reckon I ain't got but a few years left in me and I fer sure in shitcakes ain't gonna live 'em alone if I don't have to." Granny stood and faced Abram, hands on her hips. "I done lost my daughter 'cause of my stubborn pride. If Maggie says yer the man she wants, then I'm gonna have to accept that. I know ya got a good heart, but ya better treat her right or ya'll answer to me."

"What are you saying, Granny?"

"I'm tellin' ya. Fix things between my granddaughter and ya."

Stop running from the future, Abram. Run to it. Run to Maggie.

Abram wasn't positive if the words in his mind were his or Granny's. He intended to assure the old woman that *things* between him and Maggie would work out, but fear clogged the words in his throat and all he managed was a nod.

She patted his thigh. "Ya ain't one of us, but I reckon ya'll do."

Chapter Fourteen

"Howdy, Devane."

Abram glanced up from his position on the ground outside Granny's porch. Sullivan Mooreland stood a few feet away. Grinning.

"Heard Granny O'Neil was putting in a crapper, and I had to see it with my own eyes." Sullivan nodded to the huge box near Abram's feet. "What kind of toilet is that?"

"Centrex 2000." With Jo Mooreland's permission, Abram had researched toilets online using one of the school's computers and had found a model he believed would work in Granny's cabin. Yesterday UPS had delivered the toilet to the post office in Finnegan's Stand. After retrieving the commode, he'd read the instructions in his Jeep, then made a quick trip into the hardware store to purchase the tools required to install the system.

Mooreland edged closer, dropped to his knees and studied the unit. "How does the thing work without a hookup to a sewage line?"

"It's a one-pint flush toilet that has a three-inch plumbing pipe that connects to a composting unit under the deck. The unit itself is electrical, so as long as

Granny has 110-volt electricity, the heater in the concealed compartment directs the odors up a vent pipe and out the side of the cabin."

"Amazing."

"This kind of toilet is common in cabins and seasonal homes," Abram explained.

"What about drainage?"

Shifting awkwardly to a sitting position, Abram said, "An overflow security drain is connected to the unit for times of heavy use." He nodded to the hole he'd dug a few feet away. "That's the drain pit. It's filled with gravel and covered with dirt. I'll cap it with a plastic lid and that should handle the overflow from the unit."

"Want any help?"

Surprised by the offer, Abram didn't respond immediately.

"Listen," Sullivan said. "I haven't heard what happened between you and Maggie, but Granny's been whining to Jo every day that she misses her granddaughter. Any chance you two will work things out?"

Did everyone in the clan consider him and Maggie a couple? Abram was a private man and generally didn't make a habit of discussing his affairs with others. He'd rarely opened up to the men in his unit in Iraq, although he'd always been available to listen to his soldiers vent their woes.

You're no longer in Iraq. You don't have to put on a brave front and act as if nothing is wrong with your life. "I guess it's up to Maggie," he answered honestly.

"So the toilet installation is a stall tactic?" Mooreland nodded to the assortment of parts and tools scattered across the grass and dirt.

A stall tactic? Had he unconsciously volunteered to

help Granny in order to gain more time to gather the courage needed to go after Maggie? *Yes.* Because a part of him remained unsure his love was enough to keep Maggie with him for better or worse. For forever.

"Maggie's a great catch."

Abram met Sullivan's gaze. "Yes, she is." Maggie was a natural caregiver and Abram had to be certain Maggie didn't stay with him out of pity or obligation. Even if they got beyond those issues as a couple, Abram's PTSD sat between them like a 69-ton behemoth army tank. What if he never conquered the disorder? What if the dreams went away for short periods, then resurfaced? Maggie was entitled to more than a lifetime of his mood swings and nightmares.

And what if one day she's had enough and wants to leave? Watching Maggie walk away would kill him. Even now, he missed her like hell.

Mooreland broke into Abram's daydreaming. "It wasn't smooth sailing for me and Jo in the beginning."

"Granny mentioned that you'd barged into the hollow uninvited and snooped around for information on a dead man." Abram chuckled. "Her words, not mine."

"Did she tell you how Jo and I met?" When Abram shook his head, Mooreland wandered over to the porch steps and sat. "I came looking for a story. Lightning Jack was a famous bootlegger and Jo's grandfather. A few years ago, he died, but Jo continued brewing his moonshine recipe and selling the liquor in his name."

Abram set his wrench aside. "Did you get your story?"

"I got a story, but not the one I came for. I left the hollow, then discovered a couple of weeks later that my boss at the newspaper had turned my information over to the DEA."

"The Drug Enforcement Administration?"

"Yeah. By the time I found out, Jo had been sitting in jail over a week. I believed for sure I'd blown it with her. Not until I realized that I might lose her did I admit how much I loved her and wanted to make a life with her and Katie."

"I had assumed Katie was yours."

"Not biologically, but in every other way, she's mine. We're pretty close, even though Jo and I haven't been married long. But that's neither here nor there. What I'm trying to say is that I never expected I'd be happy living in a *holler* in the Appalachian Mountains." He shrugged. "Now I can't imagine my life anywhere but here—where people stick their noses in my business and offer advice I never ask for."

"Amen to that," Abram concurred.

"The clan might butt into your life from time to time, but they're caring people. What's most important is Granny's approval, and you've got that if you decide to make Heather's Hollow your new home."

Humbled by Mooreland's words, Abram clenched his hands into fists. After a lengthy silence, he said, "Did Granny tell you that I gave the cabin and the land back to her?" Abram had already decided he'd move on if things didn't work out between him and Maggie. He wanted Maggie to be free to run the clinic without worrying that he lived nearby.

"Does that mean you're staying or leaving?"

"That's up to Maggie." What Abram wanted was simple: to be with Maggie. But wanting wasn't always enough. Once Maggie learned nothing stood in her way of returning to Heather's Hollow and managing the health clinic—except Abram—she'd have to make a decision—to be with him or not.

"Then go after her," Sullivan encouraged.

"Intend to as soon as I finish with the toilet." He loved Maggie with every dysfunctional cell in his body, but he was terrified of confessing his feelings to her. Save for his pride, the war had stolen everything from him. Yet he'd gladly throw aside his pride if it allowed him a second chance with Maggie.

Since Mooreland appeared to be in a talkative mood, Abram shared one of his worries with the other man. "If things work out between me and Maggie, I'm not sure how I'd support a wife and maybe kids some day if we stayed in the hollow."

A huge grin wreathed Sullivan's face. "Speaking of children…can you keep a secret?"

"Sure."

"Jo's pregnant."

A sliver of envy pricked Abram. "Congratulations." If Abram got his head screwed on straight, would Maggie consider having children with him?

"We haven't told anyone." Sullivan cut a glance to the cabin. "It's still early, so we're waiting another month, until Thanksgiving, before we share the news."

"Mum's the word," Abram promised.

"I never planned to have any kids, and now that I'm going to be a father twice—" he shrugged "—I can't wait."

The man's joy was palpable. "I hope things go as planned then," Abram offered.

"Back to the discussion of income. Your concern about supporting a family is legitimate. The clan will help."

"Are you talking charity?" Abram scowled.

"No, I'm not suggesting a handout. For a while now, Patrick Kirkpatrick, the supervisor up at the sawmill, has been considering hiring—"

"Hate to burst your bubble but…" Abram motioned to his prosthesis. "Only got one good leg."

Word must have spread about Abram's disability, because Mooreland didn't act surprised. "Last I heard, an accountant doesn't need any legs to do the job. Kirkpatrick's been taking care of the books along with running the place for the past three years and it's grown to more than he can handle."

"Then why hasn't he hired someone?"

"He wants an employee he can trust—a person who has the best interests of the clan at heart. The mill can't afford to go under. If the men lost their jobs, they'd pack up their families and leave the area."

Abram didn't mind admitting he might be interested in applying for the position, but before he said as much, Mooreland continued, "Salary might be a problem."

"Meaning?"

"Kirkpatrick can't pay a big-city salary. But I imagine you receive some sort of pension from the army that might help make up the difference."

"Thanks, I'll consider it."

"Better get back to writing. Jo and I sold our book, *Secrets of Heather's Hollow.* The manuscript is due on the editor's desk by Christmas."

"You're full of good news today."

"We're pretty excited about it, although Jo is already fretting over our first lecture tour. But that's not until next summer when the book hits store shelves."

Mooreland turned to leave, then paused. "My wife

and Granny are as close as any grandmother and grand-daughter. Granny's been a solid rock in Jo's life since she returned from college years ago. But it's Jo's fondest wish for Granny to live out her final days with her own kin at her side. Make it happen, Devane."

"You just want Granny to butt into someone else's life for a change," Abram retorted.

With a wave Mooreland retreated around the side of the cabin.

"Who's butting into whose business?"

Abram jerked sideways, his heart stalling when he spotted Maggie standing near the outhouse. *How much of his and Mooreland's conversation had she over-heard?*

"We have to talk, Abram." She charged forward, a determined glint in her eyes, her long black hair swaying across her shoulders. Like a warrior queen readying for battle, Maggie was magnificent. His heart thundered in his chest. He'd be an absolute idiot to allow this woman to slip away without a fight.

MAGGIE HOPED her show of bravado concealed how scared to death she was. Her insides shook and her pulse pounded. Her decision to leave Louisville behind and make Heather's Hollow her new home, to become a rural-clinic nurse in a community that would eventually learn everything about her, including the size of her underwear, wasn't half as intimidating as facing this seasoned soldier.

Determined to fight for Abram and the life she be-lieved they were entitled to, she swallowed the knot in her throat and took a deep breath. She had to remain calm and focused and not run off at the mouth in non-sensical tangents.

Abram wasn't helping her nerves by looking everywhere but at her. She suspected he was lining up an escape route and she recognized that her first objective was to prevent him from fleeing before she spoke her mind. Hoping to put him at ease—as relaxed as one could be when confronted with a purposeful woman—she asked, "How did you convince Granny to put in a toilet?"

His eyes widened at the question. *Good.* She'd caught him off guard. She required every advantage to win the battle of the hearts between her and Abram.

A hint of a smile played at the corners of his mouth. "She asked for the *crapper*…as she calls it."

Maggie cut a glance several yards away. "I wonder what caused her to change her mind about the outhouse she affectionately calls Aunt Susan."

"You did."

"The toilet's for me?"

"Granny misses you, Maggie. She wants you to return home."

Home. Being separated from Granny, even for a few weeks, had forced Maggie to admit she yearned to be near her grandmother for however many birthdays the old woman had left on earth. She was under no illusion that their relationship would be smooth sailing. She and Granny had a lot of painful memories to sort through as well as new memories to create.

And Maggie had brought her mother's ashes back. Now that she intended to make the hollow her home, she believed her mother would be at peace. When the time was right, Granny and Maggie would spread her mother's ashes in the labyrinth.

"Won't be easy," Abram cut into her thoughts.

Maggie had lost track of the conversation. "What won't be easy?" Was he referring to them or being around Granny?

"Living in the hollow."

Ah. They were dancing in circles. "That's true."

Maggie had enjoyed the sense of community she'd experienced during her time in the hollow, but she acknowledged drawbacks to living among the clan—Granny being the main one. There would be times the two of them would go head-to-head over their differing medical practices. Even so, Maggie belonged in the hollow as much as Granny. As much as Abram.

"Let's not talk about the hollow, Granny or her new crapper." Maggie moved forward, one slow step at a time, allowing Abram to adjust to her nearness. When his shoulders stiffened, she stopped. "I want to talk about us."

He cleared his throat. "I'm leaving the land and the cabin to Granny—for the clinic."

"That's generous."

His gaze glanced off her like a boxing punch. "I'll be done installing the toilet by the end of the day."

"Then what?" she challenged. When he didn't respond, she said, "Where will you run to next?"

A nerve along his jaw pulsed. "Does it look like I'm running?"

She'd take anger over complacency anytime with this man.

"I don't want to argue with you, Maggie."

"Why not? You're a fighter, Abram. It's in your blood. Whether you want to be or not, you'll be a soldier the rest of your life." He stared at her as if she was nuts. "Fight your PTSD. Fight for the right to live with a sense of peace and acceptance inside you. Fight to be happy again. And most important…fight for *me*."

His dark-eyed gaze swallowed her. Her chest ached at the yearning in his brown orbs. She edged forward until they stood toe-to-toe. "I don't need you to protect me from you. I need you to love me, Abram."

He studied the tips of his boots, then raised his head. His eyes shone with such desperate hope that she clenched her hands into fists to keep from reaching for him. "Maggie." Her name escaped his mouth in a hoarse whisper.

"Wait." She held up a finger. "Before you decide to say things to drive me away, you should know that I've thought a lot about us and the challenges we'll face as a couple if we stay together. I acknowledge it won't always be comfortable." She swallowed. "You must believe me when I tell you that I don't want to be with you out of a sense of pity. Yes, I'm a nurse and nurses are nurturing people. I admit it hurts to watch you struggle with your disability—I wouldn't be human if I didn't wish you hadn't had to experience losing your leg. But I'm not repulsed by your injury. She looked deep in his eyes and willed him to believe her. "I love you, Abram. All of you. You might be a battle-worn soldier, but deep inside you're a good, decent man. Otherwise you'd never have blamed yourself for the deaths of those under your command."

"I'm not sure I'll ever put that behind me, Maggie. Or that I'll ever be well—" he pointed to his head "—here."

"You will, Abram, but only if you allow yourself to.

Your men would want you to go on with life—out of respect for the sacrifices they and their families have made. There will always be questions and what ifs. But mixed in with the uncertainty will be heartwarming memories of those soldiers. The memories and my love and support will heal you."

"Are you through?" he asked.

"No." She cupped his strong jaw, smoothing her fingertips over his lips. "Making love with you was wonderful, Abram. All I ever dreamed it would be. And I won't lie to you and say I don't want a family, because I do. I want babies. With you. But if it takes time for you to get to that point, that's okay. I'm not in a hurry."

His left eyebrow lifted. "Finished?"

Suddenly she lost her voice. But she managed a nod.

"Now I have a few things to say." His gaze softened as it roamed over her face. "I love you, Maggie."

She had been certain Abram had feelings for her, but hearing him voice them brought such an intense surge of relief, her eyes flooded with tears.

"I never fought as hard against an enemy as I fought against my feelings for you." He wiped a tear that dribbled from her eye. "I don't deserve you, but damned if I can help myself from wanting you. Loving you." His chest shuddered. "If we travel this road together, I guarantee it will be filled with potholes and detours. But I trust you, Maggie O'Neil, to steady me and keep me moving forward."

She wrapped her arms around his neck. "I'm far from a perfect catch."

His eyes shone with humor. "How so?"

"If you marry me, Granny will meddle in our affairs."

"How much damage can one eccentric old—"

"I hear ya yakkin' 'bout me," Granny's voice interrupted. Maggie's grandmother stepped onto the porch and squinted through the screen. "So what's it gonna be, soldier boy. Ya makin' a decent woman out of my granddaughter or not?"

Abram cuddled Maggie. "With your permission I'd like to marry your granddaughter."

"Ya gonna treat her right and make her happy?"

"I'll do my best."

"Ya gonna give her babies? I ain't gettin' any younger and I expect to hold my great-grandchild afore I meet my Maker."

"We'll do our best to give you a great-grandchild."

"Ya plannin' to live here in the holler, 'cause if yer goin' to the city, then I'm a comin' with ya. I ain't losin' another daughter."

Abram gazed into Maggie's eyes. "You okay with moving into the cabin until we build a house of our own?"

For the first time since her mother's death, Maggie felt at peace. "Yes." She rose on tiptoe and kissed Abram's mouth, not caring that her grandmother observed.

When the kiss ended, Abram answered, "We're staying, Granny."

"Good. Now, get back to workin' on my crapper. Maggie, git in here and help me. I'm experimentin' with a recipe for ringworm. Annie's boys come down with it again." The old woman disappeared inside.

"Are you sure about us?" Abram cupped Maggie's face and stared into her eyes.

"More than sure."

"I love you." He gathered her close, his mouth brushing hers, sealing their future with a kiss.

This was right where Maggie belonged—in her soldier's arms.

* * * * *

Look for the final book in Marin Thomas's
Hearts of Appalachia miniseries
A COAL MINER'S WIFE
Available August 2008
Only from Harlequin American Romance

HARLEQUIN® *Romance*®

MEDITERRANEAN DADS

In the first of this emotional Mediterranean Dads duet, nanny Julie is whisked away to a palatial Italian villa, but she feels completely out of place in Massimo's glamorous world. Her biggest challenge, though, is ignoring her attraction to the brooding tycoon.

Look for

The Italian Tycoon and the Nanny

by Rebecca Winters

in March wherever you buy books.

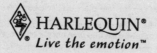

HARLEQUIN®
Live the emotion™

www.eHarlequin.com

HRI7500

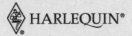

HARLEQUIN®

American ★ Romance®

COMING NEXT MONTH

#1201 THE GENTLEMAN RANCHER by Cathy Gillen Thacker
Texas Legacies: The Carrigans

When Taylor O'Quinn left Texas to pursue a writing career, Jeremy Carrigan missed his former best friend more than she'd ever know. Seeing her again makes him want more than just the camaraderie they used to share. Can he convince the now famous novelist to help a certain doctor-turned-gentleman-rancher stay put in Laramie—as Jeremy's friend, lover and wife?

#1202 GOIN' DOWN TO GEORGIA by Ann DeFee

Magnolia Bluffs, Georgia, looks like the perfect small Southern town. But big-city detective Zack Maynard smells trouble brewing below the surface with a real estate development his family has invested in. And that means dealing with one of the company partners, Liza Henderson, a not-so-perfect small Southern woman. Although, as Zack discovers, perfection is a quality that might be seriously overrated!

#1203 AN UNLIKELY MOMMY by Tanya Michaels
Fatherhood

After growing up with a trio of overprotective brothers, Ronnie Carter is ready to break loose and live a little. But she gets more than she bargained for when she meets handsome high school teacher Jason McDeere and his irresistible toddler daughter. Although Ronnie hadn't planned on taking on a ready-made family, Jason and Emily are rapidly turning the town mechanic's mind to motherhood…

#1204 THE PILOT'S WOMAN by Ann Roth

When D. J. Hatcher helps Liza Miller board his seaplane, it's déjà vu for both of them. Three years ago D.J. flew the jilted bride home. Now she's coming back to beautiful Halo Island—but is it to stay? Liza seems reluctant to start a relationship with a man who has also been burned by love. Do the sultry breezes and sizzling sunsets portend romance…and second chances?